I slid to the floor an[...] [...] as black as a hat. I s[...] kept going, a hand on either wall. The living room door was open. I skirted the sofa, knocked my other toe, felt for the telly and put my hand out for the conservatory door. It was open.

'Sam?'

And then it happened.

The patio was suddenly illumined by a white-blue light. Moonlight, I thought at first. But it was coming from the ground.

In the light I could see Sam, leaning forward in his chair, opening the outside door.

'Sam – don't – too cold—'

He didn't hear, which wasn't surprising because my voice was soundless. I started forward, but my bashed toes seemed not to move on the carpet. I was only halfway across the conservatory when Sam got the outer door open. At the same time, right at his feet, there was an enormous gout of steam, pale silver, ethereal, and the train emerged . . .

SUSAN SALLIS

NO TIME AT ALL

CORGI BOOKS

NO TIME AT ALL
A CORGI BOOK 0 552 52813 7

First publication in Great Britain

PRINTING HISTORY
Corgi edition published 1994
Corgi edition reprinted 1994

Set in 11/14pt Monotype Plantin by
Phoenix Typesetting, Ilkley, West Yorkshire

Corgi Books are published by Transworld Publishers Ltd,
61– 63 Uxbridge Road, Ealing, London W5 5SA,
in Australia by Transworld Publishers (Australia) Pty Ltd,
15– 25 Helles Avenue, Moorebank, NSW 2170,
and in New Zealand by Transworld Publishers (NZ) Ltd,
3 William Pickering Drive, Albany, Auckland.

Printed and bound in Great Britain by
Cox & Wyman Ltd, Reading, Berkshire

For Bubby
With all my love

One

I'll start with that first night in the new house. Bungalow. We moved there because of Sam's wheelchair, so there was no upstairs and no cellar like in the old house. It could have easily happened in the old house. But not in a newly built bungalow with no crooks and crannies. But it did.

Sam was on the bottom bunk and we had my dressing-gown cord between us as usual. Sam called it our telephone. We had a code. One pull: good night. Two pulls: wake up. Unless I slept through the alarm, there were never two pulls. Sam could see to himself in the night like he did in the day. Sam was the most independent kid brother anyone ever had.

So when a yank on my wrist woke me out of a dream where I was driving the latest Advanced Passenger Train around a series of bends that had the suspension keeling right over at an angle of practically forty-five degrees, I was instantly awake, hanging over the side of my bunk, hissing, 'What's up?'

Sam's answering whisper was a deliberate thread of sound in the intensity of dark.

'Just listen.'

I listened, squeezing my eyes tight then opening them wide. That was my latest technique for waking up. It was good.

Sam snapped sibilantly, 'For Pete's sake! Stop breathing!'

'Excuse me,' I whispered back, heavily sarcastic. But I did hold my breath and then stopped squeezing my face up in case that was squeaking or something.

And I heard it.

It was a rumble. Coming down the lane from the village. It came and went. When it went I said, 'Car.'

Sam said, 'No engine noise. It's behind the farm. Wait till it gets nearer.'

I waited. I never let Sam tell me what to do just because of the wheelchair. But he's pretty sensible for a kid who still believes in magic.

The rumble came again. It wasn't something you hear with your ears. It kind of came up from the floor into the bunks.

'What on earth is it?' I asked.

Sam said, 'Idiot. It's a train.'

I squeezed my eyes shut. Was I still in my dream? I fumbled for the controls of the Advanced Passenger Train and knotted my duvet cover in my hands.

The rumble shuddered ever so gently under the house where there was no cellar and then was in the garden. At exactly the same time, the foghorn out in the Channel moaned.

I hissed triumphantly, 'There! It's a ship! That throbbing note . . . it's a ship!'

'It's a train,' Sam stated positively in the maddening way he had. 'It's a steam train. It's Grandad's old train.'

That settled it. Grandad had been a railway buff and had lost all his money in buying a private line after the railways were nationalized back in the dark ages. Also, Grandad had been dead for three years.

'For Pete's sake,' I whispered in disgust. 'Go back to sleep!'

And I rolled over and felt for the controls of the APT. She was there, waiting for me, and as I built up her speed to 150 miles per hour, she whistled. All by herself she whistled.

It sounded exactly like one of the old steam-train whistles that Grandad had had on record and video.

We'd always lived in Bristol; in a tall thin house in Totterdown where we had to carry Sam and the wheelchair up and down stairs all the time. Grandad had his train layout in the attic and he knew most of the people in the engine sheds at Temple Meads. So what with the station and the attic we had plenty to do. Dad said we were brainwashed. We were happy. I didn't mind school too much and though Sam hated his school, he wasn't there often because of his chest.

Then Grandad died and Dad was made redundant and everything fell to pieces.

When the council wanted to buy up our terrace to widen the road, Mum said this was our chance to make a new start. The doctor reckoned Sam's chest would improve if we could get out of the city and there was a really good special school at Kingscote, right on the coast.

She was in her 'think positive' mood. And it really worked. Dad got a job as caretaker for the school in Kingscote and the man who had built the bungalow in a village near the sea wall went bankrupt, so we got it at a good price. You could smell the sea from the garden. You could have seen it if it hadn't been for the sea wall which the Italian prisoners of war had built to stop the floods. But the best thing was, although it was so neat and manageable, it had this big conservatory on the side where we could put Grandad's trains.

'It's all meant!' Mum said, grinning from ear to ear.

Dad said, 'You're just like your father. The eternal optimist.'

'And what's wrong with that?' Mum asked aggressively. 'You always look on the dark side! Someone's got to see the silver lining in the clouds!'

And Dad grinned because he usually does when Mum tells him off. Then he said in a soppy voice, 'I love it when you're angry.'

And she started to giggle, and the next minute they're kissing. I rolled my eyes at Sam and he rolled his back.

The next morning I realized the train had been a dream.

'We've never shared a dream before,' Sam said doubtfully.

'There's a first time for everything,' I came back. Dad says I talk in clichés, whatever that might mean. But Grandad always used to say there was a first time for everything and that was what made life exciting.

'True.' Sam looked disappointed for a moment, then smiled. 'True,' he said again and levered himself expertly into his wheelchair. 'And it's my turn to be first in the bathroom!' He twirled his chair and was gone before I could untie my half of the 'telephone' and unwrap the duvet.

So I tidied up the bunks and put some more stuff away in the fitted cupboards and thought how odd it was to be able to hear Mum and Dad talking in the kitchen, and while I was at it I pulled out some of the drawers and felt around the floorboards underneath. It was silly really; I don't know why I did it. There were no hidden trapdoors; not even a loose board.

I shoved the drawers back again and went to shout through the bathroom door at Sam.

Dad called from down the hall, 'No hurry, Matt. The kettle's on the blink and there's no milk.'

But Mum was right behind him.

'First day of the holidays, boys! And the sun is shining! You can fetch the milk from the farm while I boil some water in a saucepan!'

So that's what we did. By the time I'd shown my face some soap and water, Sam was dressed and ready to go. And it was just great. The lane would be a mess in winter, but now all the cowpats made a cushioned surface for Sam's chair and we raced along between the tall hedgerows and watched a flotilla of ducks swimming in the ditch and waited for a gaggle of geese to cross the farmyard before we knocked on the door.

Mrs Price beamed at us as she poured milk into a jug.

'Don't forget to bring your own jug tomorrow, my little flowers,' she said dotingly – people talk like that when they see Sam's chair. 'Just let it settle for a minute or two and you'll have thick cream on top for your cereal.'

'Yum,' said Sam because he knew it was expected.

I said, 'Thank you very much, Mrs Price.'

She tucked a carton of eggs into the bag on the side of the wheelchair and put her fingers to her lips.

'Why did she do that?' Sam asked on the way back.

'It's a present,' I explained.

'She's nice,' Sam said. 'Just like an apple dumpling.'

'*That's* where I've seen her before,' I said, striking my forehead.

Sam crowed, 'On your plate in a pool of custard!'

And we laughed all the way back up the lane.

It was going to be great living in Little Kingscote.

If it had been wet, we were going to start setting up Grandad's trains. But as it was a real July morning, we explored while Mum and Dad went on unpacking and sorting.

The garden was just part of the field, bounded on two sides by the tall thick blackberry hedges that lined the lane, and by the sea wall on the other. There was a lot of sky because we were right in the middle of the Somerset Levels. After Totterdown it was amazingly flat. Sam was going to be able to bowl along for miles without help. He needed a shove to get up the steep side of the sea wall though. But once on top there was a tarmac path which ran all the way to the Old Priory.

'This is great!' he yelled into the enormous spaces around us. 'Great! D'you hear me, sky? I'm part of you now! Great!'

Automatically I said, 'Shut up!' But beneath us

in the garden, trying to rig up a clothes line, Mum called, 'Go on, Sam! Yell as loud as you like! The cows won't mind and it'll stretch your lungs!'

So Sam yelled his head off and Mum laughed and Dad came out to see what it was all about and I did a war-dance on top of the sea wall. It really was going to be great living in Little Kingscote.

That afternoon, Dad started lifting the turf to make a paved area where Sam would be able to go when the hard earth turned to mud. I rolled the plates of turf and put them in a wheelbarrow and trundled around to the front where Mum was trying to make a lawn over the builders' rubble. Sam sat on the warm dry earth beneath the grass and picked up the stones so that we could lay paving slabs. He was in his daydreaming mood. He'd pick up a stone and hold it in his hand for ages, turning it round and staring at it from different angles. I noticed he was putting some of them in his pocket. He was the craziest kid.

But between us we made a green patch either side of the front door and a level area at the back where Mum could stand to peg out clothes and Sam could spin his chair. He could only do that in the playground in Bristol. It was worth seeing. He could tilt and spin his chair on either wheel.

'I'll make a few enquiries about paving stones,' Dad said, leaning on his spade and surveying the gash we'd made in the field. 'We could have it done by the end of the week, Matt. Weather permitting.'

I hadn't seen Dad so enthusiastic for ages.

Sam was a bit quiet. But he ate two cheese sandwiches for tea which was good.

Mum said, 'What did I tell you? Our luck has changed.'

Dad said, 'Too right. You'll love your new school, Sam. And we can go together and come home together.'

I felt a qualm then, wondering what *my* new school would be like. But it was only July and school didn't start till September.

The 'telephone' rang that night again. This time it wasn't quite so dark and I could see the clock. Just past midnight.

'What's up?' I asked again.

'It's the train!' Sam said excitedly.

I listened. The rumble came up the long posts of the bunks and into the elbow on which I was leaning. And then was gone. I waited for the foghorn. Nothing.

'It's some machinery down at the farm. We'll ask the apple dumpling tomorrow when we get the milk.'

'It's a train,' Sam said. And then, 'Look.'

He reached under his pillow and held out his hand. Two long bolts lay on his small palm.

I stared at them.

'So?'

'I found them in the garden.'

'So?'

'They're for bolting the fishplates into the rails.'

Fishplates are the metal pieces that hold railway lines into position at each join.

'You don't know that,' I said flatly.

'I do,' Sam replied.

We could have gone on like that all night, so I reverted to being caustic.

'So?'

'So there was a railway running through our garden.'

I snorted. I told you he was a crazy kid.

As I drifted back into a decent dreamless sleep, I heard that blasted whistle again.

Two

This book is really about Sam, not about me, but I'll have to come into it a lot because it happened mostly when Sam and I were together. And in spite of being such a great basketball player and so independent he'd put his fists up to me at times, he was still what they call paraplegic, so there were times when I had to take over for him. Not only that, but because he sat in a wheelchair all day, he got awful chest infections. He'd had pneumonia twice.

I was fourteen at that time and Sam was ten. I expect there were moments when those four years separated us, but I can't remember when they were. We just met on middle ground most of the time; either Sam became fourteen or I became ten or we both became twelve! And like I said, life had been a bit grim for a while, but being at the bungalow made up for everything. It was great. We became sort of detectives. And we solved our case. That's what the book is about. Sam and me being detectives and solving our case.

That last week in July was hot. Really hot. Although it was school holidays, Dad had to go in to the special school where he was caretaker and do some painting and spring-cleaning. So we all went. It was good for Sam to get to know what the place looked like; good for Mum too, I expect. She nosed around like a bloodhound, especially in the gym. There were walking bars and trampolines and a basketball court and a pile of mats – everything.

Dad said, 'The kids roll on the mats, apparently. Strengthens the arms and they just love it – laugh all the time.'

Sam said, 'Have they got a decent basketball team?' Sam has visions of being chief shooter in the paraplegics' team.

'A first and second.' You'd have thought Dad was headmaster the way he talked. 'They played four matches last term apparently. Two home. Two away. Won three.'

Sam made a face.

Dad nodded. 'Should have been four. They need you, old man.'

They laughed and started hand-slapping and Mum and me rolled our eyes and sleeves and began washing the floor of the gym. Sam was going to help Dad to emulsion the walls. We had a great time. In the afternoon, after we'd had our sandwiches, the headmaster looked in. He was called Mr Barker; Dad had told us he was really nice and didn't even mind that the kids called him Bow-wow. 'Better than Rottweiler,' he'd said, grinning.

He shook Sam's hand.

'Glad to have you, Sam,' he said as if Sam was thirty-five. 'Good of you to help out with the cleaning.'

'I like it.' Sam had quite a lot of emulsion on his overall but Mr Barker didn't make any joky comments about that. Instead, he told him about two or three kids who were Sam's age. 'They've gone away for the summer, otherwise I'd get you together. Lisa Jenkins, who runs the tuck shop, will be home at the end of the week. She's fifteen. I'll let your dad have her address and if you want to know anything about Automobiles, get in touch.'

Sam looked. Dad said, 'I forgot to tell you, Sam. This place isn't known as Kingscote Special School. It's called Automobiles.'

'We named it ourselves,' Mr Barker explained. 'We're all mobile. And some of us are auto. Electric chairs.'

Sam looked again. His physio told him yonks ago that an ordinary chair helped his biceps as well as his lungs.

Mr Barker did not enlarge on the subject. He asked if we were settling in at Little Kingscote, and when Dad told him how we'd started on the patio he said he'd phone a friend of his who knew someone who supplied paving stones. Then he admired the walls again and went away.

Dad said, 'He knew we'd be here. His way of meeting the family.'

Mum was appreciative. She'd had enough of

sitting the other side of a desk for an 'informal chat'.

Anyway, Mr Barker's friend of a friend turned up the next morning and said he'd got some flagstones left over from a big order the other side of Bristol and we could have them at cost and he'd get his two sons to help with the laying.

By the end of that first week, the back of the house looked wonderful. Mum treated herself to a 'whirly' clothes line and when she wasn't drying clothes she pegged old sheets around it and it was the kind of tent a wheelchair could get in and out of. At the other end of the patio, Dad put up a basket so that Sam could practise. And when the tide was right we edged the chair cautiously along a small jetty which ran from the sea wall, and chucked out a line baited with bits of bread. We never caught anything, but we liked to think that one day we would.

There was so much to do we almost forgot about the 'noises off'. Or perhaps we got used to them. I woke at midnight most nights and waited almost idly for the rumbling to begin. I knew Sam was awake too, though he never pulled the telephone cord. The funny thing was, we never mentioned the noises to Mum and Dad. Maybe we thought they'd worry that the house foundations weren't sound. Maybe we simply liked having the noises all to ourselves.

Then, towards the end of August, as I squatted

on the jetty by Sam's chair and watched our float gliding on the surface several metres away, he suddenly brought up the subject.

'They're connected, you know.'

'Connected? The float and the bait d'you mean. 'Course they are, idiot.'

'No-o-o. Double idiot.'

I glanced up at him. He was wearing a baseball cap which was printed with the name 'Rambo' just above its peak. It was very hot and Mum had supplied us with a golfing umbrella to protect us. It was rolled up and stuck in the side of the chair. Of course.

'Sun getting to you?'

'Treble idiot. I mean the train noise and the fishplate bolts.'

I'd known that was what he meant; like I said, we hadn't talked about our noises much, and I wasn't particularly keen on having a discussion about them now.

'Train noises, my foot. It's shipping. Going up to Avonmouth. Told you that before.'

He totally ignored me.

'The train runs on a proper line. Somewhere.'

I twitched and the float bobbed in reply. It was that word, 'somewhere'. Sam knew it too.

'Well, it's not anywhere we can see, is it?' he asked reasonably.

I squinted up at him again. He was one of those kids who could play pretend games all by himself without moving at all. Well, he'd had to, I suppose, being stuck in a wheelchair all his life.

I decided to play along.

'So where d'you think it could be?' I asked.

He looked down at me. His hair, bunched down by the baseball cap on top, sprang around his ears like a girl's. I'd tell Mum he must have a haircut.

'You being sarky?' he said belligerently.

'No!' I hadn't been. 'No. I just wondered . . . what you thought.'

'I don't know, do I?' His eyes were very bright blue when he was angry. 'That's what you've got to find out!'

'Me?'

'Well, I can't dig, can I? You've got to start digging the garden and see what you can find.'

'Come on, Sam! This is my holiday, you know!'

'Tell Dad you're digging a garden path.' He smiled at me warmly. 'You can do it, Matt. Just an hour a day. See what turns up.'

I held his gaze for about two more seconds.

'Oh . . . OK,' I said.

And – like a reward – the float disappeared. We reeled frantically. It was a conger. It would have been big enough to cook too, but Sam made me throw it back.

Dad was amazed.

'I can't afford to get you a bike,' he said warily when I suggested the path.

'I don't need a bike. You're taking me in to school.' If I had a bike I wouldn't have to run to keep up with Sam's chair and he enjoys making me run. Says it's good for me.

'It's something we can leave till next year.' Dad looked at the field grass beyond the patio. 'We don't actually need a path.'

'No. But if I started to dig it out . . .' I stood by the window with him. 'Look – there's been a path or something there before. You can see a kind of line in the grass.'

'Yes. A cart track. There's a gap in the hedge down there. Probably there was a gate.' Dad clapped me on the shoulder. 'Do what you like, Matt. If you're interested in gardening you can take it over.'

'Well . . .' Then I saw he was grinning and shadow-boxed him into the hall.

Mum shouted, 'Will you two get in here and have your tea!'

We went in and Sam grinned his congratulations at me. Life was pretty good.

Three days later I started turning up small cubes of wood.

'Kids' building blocks?' I said to Sam.

'Wood's too rough.' He looked at me. 'You know what they are, Matt.'

I did. Grandad had told us just how a railway line was laid. The sleepers went down on a bed of ballast, then the steel chairs that held rails

23

were bolted on to the sleepers, then the rails were slotted into the chairs and firmed into place by wedges of wood. Like children's building blocks. And where rail met rail, they were joined by a piece of metal called a fishplate.

We looked down at the small pile of wedges. They were even flattened on one side where the ganger's iron mallet had hammered them home.

Sam said with quiet satisfaction, 'It is a train, Matt.'

Three

We took the first of the blackberries to Mrs Price because she was always giving us cream and things.

'Mum says we've got time to pick and you haven't,' Sam explained, handing over the plastic box solemnly.

Mrs Price was all flustered. The cream had really been for Sam, to build him up, and she didn't want to take anything in return.

'Reaching over the ditch and going headfirst in . . .' she scolded, holding the box in front of her as if it was holy. 'You could get some nasty scratches from them brambles.'

I kept well back. This was between Mrs Price and Sam.

'I don't think I'll do that.' He spoke indulgently as if to a small child. He smiled at her. 'It's my legs that don't work. Not my brain.'

I've heard him say that to people so that they went red and almost ran away. But Mrs Price was sort of . . . innocent.

'You brave little man,' she said, and before Sam could take offence she lunged forward and kissed him.

I almost laughed out loud. It was Sam who backed off this time. As soon as we were out of sight in the lane, he stopped and scrubbed furiously at his cheek.

'Serves you right,' I told him unsympathetically. 'You only say that to frighten people. She beat you at your own game.'

Sam said, 'But I like her. Or I did!'

'Then you should watch what you say.' I stopped laughing and took the chair. 'Otherwise I might have to tip you into the ditch headfirst!'

I belted down the lane with him whooping his head off, and Mum met us at the gate, grumbling but grinning.

'Noisy so-and-so's. Disturbing the peace of the countryside!' She opened the gate for us. 'That girl phoned you, Sam.'

'Girl?' His eyes nearly popped out.

'Lisa. Mr Barker mentioned her, don't you remember?'

'What did she want?'

'Only to say hello. She'll ring again.' Mum went ahead into the house. 'Let's have elevenses on our new terrace. Won't be able to sit outside much longer. Autumn's coming.'

Sam looked at me. 'I don't want the autumn to come, do you?'

'Not really.' I watched him manoeuvre expertly through the conservatory and on to the patio. He hadn't liked the girl phoning him, I knew that. I wouldn't like it either. We were in a magic circle here; we didn't want intruders.

'School,' he said glumly.

'Yeah. And rain.'

Mum followed us out. 'And maybe snow. We can set up Grandad's trains and watch the weather. Make a list of the birds we see.'

Mum was a great one for making lists. But Sam was not to be sidetracked by promises of trains and lists.

He said, 'I wish this summer could go on for ever.'

For some reason Mum suddenly looked frightened. And Dad, coming up the track that was to be our garden path, said quickly, 'Then we must make sure it does, mustn't we?'

The rain started that afternoon and was still falling two days later. Lisa Jenkins did not phone again and though Sam was pleased in one way, he wasn't in another.

'School,' he would say, watching the rain sluicing the conservatory windows.

We went into Kingscote and while Dad got the boiler going at Automobiles, Mum took us to get our school ties and have haircuts. Sam had one umbrella and Mum and I shared the other. Every now and then it tipped water down our coat collars. We weren't happy.

When we got back to Automobiles, we could hear Dad talking to someone in the hall.

'He's good at basketball,' he was saying. Mum and I exchanged grins. Dad reckons he never boasts about his family.

A female voice came back, hard as a nutmeg grater.

'Well, he would be, wouldn't he?'

I watched Mum's grin disappear and knew mine too had been wiped from my face. We were used to people being bowled over by Sam's expertise with a ball and a basket. Sam himself sat very still in his chair. He was drier than we were, his new haircut making him look older than he really was. He leaned forward slightly, listening.

Dad spoke thoughtfully, not a bit aggressively – he sometimes gets aggressive about Sam when he thinks we're not listening.

'Not necessarily. Think about it.'

The female was silent, obviously thinking about it. Then she came back as abrasively as before.

'OK. But he has certain advantages.'

We waited for Dad to explode. The silence went on and on. Then at last he said, very quietly and simply, 'Yes.'

Sam crashed his chair at the swing door and bowled into the hall. We were right behind him.

Dad was standing next to an electric wheelchair. The occupant had bright red hair as coarse as rusty nails. That's all we could see.

Dad turned and smiled at us with evident relief.

'Here they are. Drowned rats. Or skinned rabbits.' He came to us, ruffled our haircuts, pecked Mum. The wheelchair stayed where it was, backed up.

Dad said, 'Lisa's grandfather brought her round. To meet you.' He went back to the electric wheel-chair. 'Lisa, this is my wife, Peggy, and my two sons, Matt and Sam. This is Lisa Jenkins.'

There was a whirr from the motor and the chair turned. She was one of the strangest-looking girls I'd ever met. Her hair stuck out at all angles and her face was the same; sharp and pointed with a long nose and a pursed mouth, a pugnacious jaw and enormous angry brown eyes. A vixen. But at least it was her face you noticed first; perhaps that was why she'd got someone to have a go at her hair with nail scissors. Because below her face her arms ended at her elbows and her legs at her knees.

Mum gripped my arm like a vice and I managed not to make a sound. Sam stayed where he was, his hands, his precious hands, on the driving wheels of his chair.

The girl, Lisa, said, 'You were listening.'

Sam said in a small voice, 'Yes.'

She laughed. 'They say eavesdroppers never hear any good of themselves.'

Sam swallowed visibly. There had been kids much worse off than him at his last school. But never anyone so angry about it before.

There was a horrible pause. The girl was smiling, thinking she'd got Sam exactly where she wanted him. And then he did something only Sam could do. He took his hands off the wheels and held them out, looking at them as if he'd never seen them before.

Then he said slowly, 'But you were right. I should be good at basketball.' And he smiled at her, his huge toothy smile. And he said, 'Thank you, Lisa.' Then he moved his chair closer to hers and said, 'There was a kid at my last school who had an artificial arm.'

She was stunned. You could see her reassembling her thoughts to accept this upstart. And then the swing doors opened again and an old man stood there. He looked about a hundred.

She stabbed one of her stumps on to the arm of her chair and it moved sharply away.

'I've got one of those. Of course. And I'm good with it.' She came to a halt by the old man and looked back at Sam. And suddenly she too grinned. 'I didn't wear it today. I wanted to show off. Gramps says I'm always showing off. Don't you, Gramps?'

Until that moment he had looked a miserable old man, absolutely unlike our Grandad who was always laughing and talking nineteen to the dozen. But then, when Lisa looked up at him, his face cracked open in a grin. 'Little Perisher,' he said, and he sounded really proud of her as if showing off and being a little perisher were the best things in the world.

Then he glanced at us. 'Got the car outside. Expect we'll meet again.'

They went. And the gym felt very empty.

Four

My school was every bit as horrible as I had known
it would be. The girls giggled and were friendly;
the boys acted as if I had rabies. It was great to
see our big old Vauxhall waiting discreetly down
the road with Sam grinning from the back seat and
Mum sitting by Dad in the front.

'I had some shopping to do,' she explained before
I could ask.

Sam said, 'She was worried about us. Mr Price
brought her in with some calves.'

I knew Mum was worried about Sam, but I
still hoped no-one from Year Ten would see me
gathered back into the bosom of my family. I slid
right down in the seat.

Mum skipped all the questions and went into
one of her 'positive' spiels.

'It's bound to be awful at first. They've got to
sniff you out. But by this time next week . . .'

I thought of Tuesday, Wednesday, Thursday,
Friday. Then the bliss of the weekend and the
horror of next Monday. I said nothing.

'And we'll start getting Grandad's trains set up
these evenings,' Dad said, catching sight of me in

the mirror, hunched down. 'If this rain keeps up, we'll be pretty well pinned down in the house.'

Sam said, 'Hey! Great!'

I looked at him. He was much too small for ten years old, which was probably why his grin looked so enormous.

'Went OK?' I asked.

He reversed his grin quickly. 'Dinners – yuk! Spelling – double yuk! Maths not bad. Art not bad.'

'Basketball?' I queried.

The grin started to bend upwards. 'Not bad,' he admitted.

'What about the other kids?'

The grin went wild. 'Not bad,' he said again.

'Lisa Jenkins had done a beachcombing project over the holiday,' Dad enlarged.

'Beachcombing?' I pushed myself up a few centimetres. 'How did she get her wheelchair on to the shingle?' The beaches were all shingle at Kingscote.

Sam contained his giggles with difficulty. 'It was while they were on holiday. She and her gramps. She lives with her gramps and he has no control over her.' He spoke almost reverently.

Dad said, 'She needs a firm hand, I'm afraid.' He met my eye in the driving mirror again and grinned unwillingly. 'It was rather funny though.'

Sam said, 'She can swim. On the sand – like commandos on their tummies, you know. And in the sea. That's how she found her – her stuff.'

'Well?' I wasn't in the mood for all this secret business.

Sam said, 'It was pants. Ladies' and men's. And she'd written a piece called "Dissertation on beachcombings of the late twentieth century".'

He could hardly get his tongue around that.

I began to feel better.

Mum said, 'It's not really funny though, is it? She's fifteen. I suppose it was amusing for others in her age group. I blame Mr Barker for allowing it to be on display to everyone.'

Sam protested vigorously. 'It was great, Mum! I couldn't read all the words but it was so *funny*! It made the first day like a – like a party!'

I thought of my first day and wished Lisa Jenkins was at the Comprehensive.

Mum was right. Of course. By the following Monday I'd been picked for the rugby Under Fourteens and the captain told me to turn up for training on Saturdays. If you're in a rugby team you've got at least fourteen mates. They might not particularly like you and you might not like them, but they're mates. It's one of those things.

The captain was eighteen and absolutely massive.

He said, 'You've got promise, Matt Savernack.'

I felt myself go red-hot.

'Thank you – er – er—' His name was Hildenborough.

'Call me Hilda,' he said kindly. 'Everyone does.'

That night as we worked at tacking down Grandad's miles of railway track, Mum said, 'Who is this Hilda? Is she pretty?'

I thought Sam would fall out of his chair with laughing.

It was another week before we put the finishing touches to the railway. Dad had made a shelf all round the conservatory on a level with Sam's wheelchair. Here and there the shelf swelled to accommodate a station or some stabling sidings or an engine shed. The shelf went across both doors so that the track was continuous.

The Prices came down for the inaugural run. Dad put bunting across the roof and played brass-band music and Sam placed the shunter on the track, switched on and marshalled a train from the engine shed: a tender, half a dozen coal wagons and a brake. He was expert at assembling a train – he'd spent hours with Grandad when he was about three. The Prices were all beaming smiles.

'Isn't he a clever darling?' Mrs Price gushed at Mum. Mum looked nervously at Sam who kept smiling somehow and purposely derailed the shunter just to show he was neither clever nor a darling.

But it was a great evening. The adults got fed-up quite soon and went into the living-room to drink sherry and chat, and Sam and I got three trains going round at once using all the sidings we had and every bit of stock.

When it was almost dark they came in to say good night.

'You've got everything so *nice*,' Mrs Price said enviously. 'No rambling great rooms to keep warm and clean, but plenty of space for the boys.'

Mr Price was chewing on an empty pipe. He looked through the conservatory windows and added his bit about the garden.

'You'll have a job if you want to get vegetables in next spring,' he said to Dad. 'Bet it was hard work digging out the patio area, wasn't it?'

'Rusty metal everywhere,' Dad agreed. 'And Matt has started on a path. Found no end of rubbish.'

Mr Price nodded and removed his pipe.

'Well, you can still see the old track, can't you? They took the rails and the sleepers but everything else was just left.'

Mrs Price and Mum were talking about bramble jelly. Sam croaked, 'Track? Rails?'

'You've heard of the old Mushroom Line, haven't you?' Mr Price looked down at him. 'Went right along by the sea. Long before them Italian prisoners of war built the sea wall. Used to be flooded every winter. But it brought coal in from Lympsham Wharf, so they kept it going as long as they could.'

I looked at Sam, then at Dad.

Dad said, 'D'you mean to tell us that the bungalow is built over a railway track?'

Old Price grinned and stabbed with the stem of his pipe.

'There was a halt just before that gate. Little Kingscote Halt.' He looked around him. 'I reckon the line must have gone right through the front bedroom and your living-room. Then under here and on to the Halt.'

Sam and I were silent.

Dad said, 'Well I'll be blowed! Hear that, boys? What would Grandad have to say about that, I wonder!'

Still we did not speak.

Mum asked what was up, and Dad and Mr Price told her. Then Mrs Price waded in with reminiscences about the train stopping so that the driver could pick mushrooms.

'It was before our time, of course,' she said. 'But some of them old stories make you laugh. The local kids used to climb into the empty coal wagons on their way back to Lympsham and turn up hours later as black as chimney sweeps!'

Mum was smiling round at everyone.

'We were meant to come here,' she said. 'And now we know what to call the bungalow.'

Dad nodded.

'Little Kingscote Halt,' he said.

I decided to play it very cool that night.

'So the mystery is solved,' I said as I climbed into my pyjamas and fastened the telephone cord to my wrist. 'All those old wedges and the fishplate bolts belonged to a real railway.'

Sam was already settled in the bottom bunk. Mum seemed to have scrubbed him rather too well that night; his face looked translucent.

'Yes, but—' he began.

I swept on regardless. 'It's great stuff, you know. Not many kids live on an old railway halt. I bet we shall turn up loads of stuff once we start digging out the path again.'

'Yes, but—'

'You could start a collection. Exhibit things. Like Lisa Jenkins!' I guffawed.

He was silent. We both knew what he wanted to say. I clambered into the top bunk and pulled the duvet up to my nose. The cord hung slack between us.

'Lights out now?' I asked.

'OK.'

I switched out the lights and the bedroom settled around us into shapes of cupboards and tables and Sam's wheelchair. The silence grew and grew till I couldn't bear it.

'Oh, for Pete's sake!' I exploded, turning on to my side. 'Why don't you just shut up!'

He didn't laugh.

I spoke with exaggerated patience. 'Look. We haven't even heard anything for the past two weeks—'

'I have.'

I exploded again. 'You rotten liar! I haven't slept a wink with worrying about school—'

'You snored! Loudly!' He too was getting angry.

I didn't deny this. Maybe that first week I had dropped off for a few seconds in between dreading the next day. And the second week I'd been exhausted enough to sleep through anything.

'Don't give me that! You haven't heard anything either!'

'I *have*!' he repeated.

'You would have pulled the cord!'

'Well, I didn't.'

'Why not?'

''Cos I was worried about you. You were having a rotten time and I—'

'I haven't said a word! I haven't grumbled! How do you know—'

'I just know.'

That shut me up.

After a bit I said, 'Have you really heard something?'

'Yes.'

'You should be sleeping. You'll be ill. You know you will.'

'No I won't. Because it doesn't take any time.'

Baffled, I stared down into the darkness of the bottom bunk.

'What on earth d'you mean by that?'

'I mean, it doesn't take up any time. From when I hear it first till it goes.'

'Oh, shut up! It goes on for ages. Like a foghorn.'

He switched on his torch and slewed sideways so that he could see me.

'I know. But I've looked at my watch when it starts. Exactly midnight. And I've looked when it stops. Exactly midnight.'

'You're dreaming.'

He didn't answer. We both knew he wasn't dreaming.

At last I lay back.

'Put out your torch and go to sleep. I'll stay awake tonight.'

'Will you?'

'Yeah.'

'Promise?'

'Promise.'

He was asleep within five minutes, I could tell from his breathing. The little devil had kept himself awake purposely to hear that blasted noise. It made me so angry. I made up my mind I'd ask the Prices tomorrow about their farm machinery. Good grief – we'd come here specially for peace and quiet!

My eyes were closing when it started up. I felt for my own torch, flicked it on and checked my watch. Like Sam said – midnight. I kept staring at those hands while the sound came closer and closer and the faint rumble came up through the long legs of the bunk beds then went on through the living-room and out into the garden.

It seemed to take for ever. But the hands on my watch were still at midnight.

I lay down and put out the torch.

The gentle sound had been somehow . . . reassuring. Rather like a steam train.

Five

Hilda yelled, 'Put more into it, Savernack!' and I stumbled across Kingscote Beach, slipping on the pebbles, pumping my arms, blowing like a whale.

Jack Martin was just ahead of me and looked over his shoulder.

'This makes press-ups seem like kids' stuff, eh, Matt?' he panted.

It did. We'd done the press-ups in the gym because it was raining – a fine misty rain that clothed the whole town in fog. Then we'd jogged down to the beach and pounded those pebbles like maniacs for the last half an hour.

Below us the tide was slipping in quietly and almost invisibly; it was four o'clock and practically dark. I thought of our living-room with the table laid for tea; Sam in the conservatory, running two trains at once, Dad watching the sport on the box, and Mum keeping an eye on everything as per usual. It was quite a prospect. Mr Price was picking me up from the school at five o'clock.

'Pick those legs *up*, Savernack!' Hilda bawled practically in my ear. 'You look as if you're sleep-walking!'

I almost was. I'd stayed awake every night for over a week now just to listen to that peculiar sound. I'd had a very cautious word with the Prices but all their machinery shut down at night. And though the blasted noise took no time at all, it kept me awake half the night wondering.

I lifted my knees almost to my chin, but still managed to catch a toe in a piece of seaweed and fall flat on my face.

'Carry on!' Hilda shouted and stood above me, looking down from his great height. It wasn't every rugby captain who would turn out with the junior team for training.

'Something up, Savernack?' he asked. 'You sick or something?'

'No . . . Hilda.' I always wanted to call him sir. 'Not sleeping, that's all.'

'Stupid kid.' He reached down. 'Get up. Have you broken anything?'

'No, sir . . . Hilda.'

'Go on up to the prom. Wait for us.' He started after the others then half turned. 'Trouble at home?'

'Oh no!'

He made a face. 'You're blooming lucky then.' And off he went.

I went up the steps to the prom and tried to calm my aching muscles by will-power. Hilda says that is quite possible. It didn't work for me.

*   *   *

43

Mr Price drove the truck as if it was made of glass. He had a new cow in the back.

'Farm over Mendip way,' he told me through the stem of his pipe. 'Gone bust. Had to split the herd and I managed to get one. I'll breed from her.'

'Good,' I said, trying to ease myself off a broken spring.

'Terrible business when a farm goes down,' Mr Price went on mournfully. 'All that equipment – tin baths – old ploughs – looks pathetic out in the rain.'

'Oh.'

'Country's in a bad way. You're old enough to know that, of course. Your dad losing his job and all.'

'He's got another one though.'

'School caretaker.'

'He prefers it. Really.'

'He's a trained engineer, Matt!'

'But we're all happier now than we were . . . before.'

He glanced sideways at me and obviously decided I wasn't old enough to understand certain things after all.

'Glad to hear it, lad. Glad to hear it.' He slowed down to five miles an hour to take a hump-backed bridge. Then said casually, 'That was the old railway bridge by the way.'

And I was reminded that I still hadn't found out . . . anything. I thought of staying awake again tonight in a vain effort to identify our noise. My bones ached. Jack Martin stayed in bed nearly all Sunday morning after training. But if I did that I'd miss out on doing things with Sam.

I left the Prices talking to their new cow and walked down the lane like a very old man.

It was October and there were still blackberries and sloes in the hedges. Somewhere in the ditches I could hear the ducks talking. But the big Somerset sky had no more warmth in it and in the dampness all around you could smell winter. I thought that tomorrow I'd shove the wheelchair on to the sea wall whatever the weather and we'd take a walk along to the jetty. We'd never been further than that. Sam wouldn't let me push him and it was hard work to manoeuvre around all the sea-wrack on the wall.

Our new house sign dangled from the gatepost. 'Little Kingscote Halt'. It made me think of Grandad and his crazy love of trains and I had to swallow suddenly. I tried not to think of Grandad too often. Sam would have liked to talk about him but I usually managed to shut him up. Grandad was a great character and when he died I thought we'd never be happy again. But we were. So maybe I'd let Sam talk about him now and then.

I opened the gate – when I'm on my own I climb the gate but I couldn't have climbed over a toadstool right then – and, parked at the side of the bungalow, was a car. Visitors. If I hadn't felt so old I'd have stayed out until they went. Gone was the dream of teatime around the fire with sport on the box. Visitors are what Dad calls 'one of life's little trials'. Mum acts as if they're royalty.

I didn't know whether it was worse or better when I discovered the visitors were Lisa Jenkins and her gramps. Better, I suppose. It could have been Uncle Harold and his wife from Bath. Then we have linen table napkins and the jam in a dish.

They were crammed into the living-room, all of them. Sam and Lisa had their chairs against the window; her gramps was sitting by Dad on the sofa, and Mum leapt up from the armchair so that I could sit down.

'I was just going to get tea anyway.' She smiled brightly at me. 'We've persuaded Mr Jenkins and Lisa to stop with us for tea. Beans on toast?'

'Smashing.' I collapsed into her chair, just stifling a groan of agony.

Lisa eyed me with disfavour. I knew she was thinking that if she had arms and legs she'd be in the kitchen helping Mum.

I said, 'Rugby training. Press-ups. Running on the beach.'

She did not say a word; just let me listen to my own tactlessness. After all, she'd probably give hundreds of pounds to be able to do press-ups and run.

Sam said proudly, 'Matt's in the third team. He's pretty good.'

Lisa said, 'Splendid. Absolutely splendid.'

I felt myself go bright red. Dad said quickly, 'Mr Jenkins was clearing out his shed. Came across some paint that might do for Automobiles.'

'I'd 'a took it round to school, but our Lisa wanted a drive,' the old man grunted. He was looking miserable again; in fact, he was looking exactly as I was feeling.

I glanced at Lisa; she was slightly pink too.

Dad said, 'I was thinking I'd paint the cloakroom at half term. That pale blue will be just the ticket.'

I remembered what old Price had said. Dad was a trained engineer. And here he was, using leftover paint to tart up a school cloakroom.

Sam leaned forward eagerly. 'I could use those stencils, Dad.' He turned to Lisa. 'I had some butterfly stencils last Christmas. They'd look good on the blue, wouldn't they?' He grinned suddenly. 'Or would you rather we painted on some knickers!'

And, most surprisingly, Lisa Jenkins went from pink to dark red. I smiled. My aches had subsided; I stood up.

'Need a hand, Mum?'

Mum was trundling in the trolley loaded with crocks.

'Just lay up then, love . . .' She fluffed a cloth over the table and closed one eye at me. The linen napkins were on the trolley. And the silver napkin rings from Grandma.

Tea would not have been too bad except that old

Mr Jenkins kept staring out of the window as if there was someone there. It made me look up too. It was the sort of thing Sam did to catch me out. I looked the old man straight in the eye and he sort of huddled down in his chair and stared at his beans instead. It was only when Sam started talking about Grandad that he seemed to recover.

'Liked trains then, did he?' he asked, smiling at Sam almost as warmly as he did at Lisa.

'He was a train buff,' Sam said proudly. And started telling old Jenkins all about the Temple Meads engine sheds and Grandad's model trains.

'Gramps used to work on the railway, didn't you, Gramps?' Lisa said, not to be outdone.

But for once she did not get that smile. His face closed up like a mousetrap and he said, 'Too long ago to remember, my girl. Much too long.' And he glanced up at the window which was now dark anyway.

After tea, Dad suggested we show Lisa the train layout. I opened the inner door carefully, let them get the chairs inside and closed it again.

'It goes right round the room, see?' Sam was like a tourist guide, flipping his chair around to indicate the up and down signals, water towers, and coal sidings.

Lisa was unexpectedly enthusiastic. She scooted round after Sam and lowered her sharp nose to gaze through tunnels and into the model houses along the track.

'My dad liked railways too,' she confided. 'Gramps won't talk about it at all, but Dad took me round the engine sheds yonks ago.'

Sam was ecstatic. 'Gosh. We might have been there at the same time!'

'Doubt it. Dad went when I was seven. You wouldn't have been born then.'

'I'm ten!' Sam protested.

'That would make you three, then.' Lisa looked at him without the scorn she used on the rest of the world. 'Yeah. I recognize you now. You were in a pushchair and you were always crying!'

Sam leaned over his knees, laughing.

She looked at me. 'I might have seen *you* there,' she said in her tough voice. 'But there were so many kids and they all look alike to me.'

I forced myself to meet her straight brown gaze. After all, she had volunteered the information about her father dying. Which meant she must trust us. Even like us.

'I never saw you,' I said. 'I wouldn't have forgotten.'

She looked away quickly and Sam said, 'Did you know this house is built on the old railway track? The one that went from Kingscote to Lympsham Wharf?'

She turned to him again.

'We wondered. When we saw the name of your house. It was called the Mushroom Line. Is that the one you mean?'

'Yes. We're trying to find out about it. But it was all torn up in the Second World War. Everyone's forgotten about it now.'

She pressed a button and moved her chair to the dark window.

'There should be something about it. Written down. Have you tried the library?'

Sam tightened his mouth. I said, 'Look. I haven't had time. I'll go there. I promise.'

Sam said. 'And pigs might fly. In any case, that won't solve the mystery.'

Lisa forgot to be angry or embarrassed. She was just surprised.

'What mystery?' she asked.

'Nothing—'

'It's still running,' Sam said.

'Don't talk such utter rubbish!' Why was I angry? Because I didn't want to look a fool in front of Lisa Jenkins?

Sam said stubbornly, 'We hear it. Every night at twelve o'clock. We hear it – it goes under the house.'

'It's machinery somewhere. Maybe a ship—'

She ignored me. 'You *hear* it?'

'And it doesn't use any time. After it's gone, it's still exactly twelve o'clock!'

'He's mad,' I told Lisa flatly. 'Absolutely stark, staring crazy—'

'No, he's not.' Lisa stared at me with those defiant eyes. 'He's the sanest person I've ever met.

If he says the Mushroom Line is still running, then it is.'

I felt she'd hit me in the solar plexus. I fought for breath.

Sam said, 'It's not a bit frightening, Lisa. In fact, it – it's – wonderful.'

Lisa looked at him thoughtfully, then at me.

At last she said kindly, 'You'd look better, Matt, if you closed your mouth.' Then to Sam: 'I might be able to help you. You see, my gramps was a signalman on the Mushroom Line. He never talks about it. You heard what he said at teatime. So there could be a mystery.'

Sam breathed, 'He was a signalman?'

'He was a bit of everything. Crossing-keeper at the Halt . . . it was only a ten-mile track.'

The door opened and Mum was there.

'It's time for you to go, Lisa. It's been so nice . . .'

Lisa smiled warmly; she looked almost pretty.

'Oh, I've enjoyed it so much, Mrs Savernack. May I come again?'

'Of course, my dear. Any time—' Mum looked straight at me as if she expected me to object.

Lisa turned that sunny smile on me.

'Leave everything in my capable and non-existent hands,' she said with all her old, virulent sarcasm.

But I didn't mind any more. Lisa Jenkins was an ally well worth having.

Six

I slept through the midnight train that night. What's more, so did Sam. Which showed we had both handed the whole problem over to Lisa. And the next day was dry and windless, a low grey sky sitting on the metallic grey sea and all the Price cows lying down, prophesying rain.

We went down for the milk before Mum and Dad were up and Mrs P. showed us the new cow, lying with the others and looking completely unruffled by yesterday's drive.

I said, 'Beats me how you know which one it is.'

Mrs Price just laughed. Sam was indignant.

'They're all different! She's got a white-eye-look.'

'So's Gertie,' I reminded him.

He was triumphant. 'See! You know who Gertie is!' He waited till Mrs Price went indoors again and said, 'You're copying Lisa!'

'Eh? What?' I didn't know what he was talking about.

'When she said yesterday that all able people look the same to her. She didn't mean it. Neither do you about the cows.' He frowned. 'Why do you both say things like that? It's not honest.'

I could have cried. Sam was so – so – transparent.

I tried to explain. 'It's just . . . sort of fooling people, I suppose.'

His frown deepened. Then he snorted. 'You're trying to be cool!'

And maybe that's what it was.

We walked for miles along the sea wall. It wasn't easy. There was a lot of rubbish on the hard tarmac top – wooden spars, barrels, piles of seaweed and even, inevitably, a shopping trolley.

The tide was going out and leaving a glistening expanse of mud. To our left, the bank dropped steeply into water meadows. And now we knew what to look for, the shorter grass and clumps of ballast showed clearly where the Mushroom Line had followed the sea down to Lympsham.

Then, unexpectedly, the tarmac ended. There was a short stretch of grass and a fence and beyond that a steep bank down to a river.

Sam said, 'Is this the coal wharf?'

'I don't think so.' I'd dragged the chair up to the fence and now I climbed on the rails to look beyond the river. 'I think I can just pick up where the line went on the other side.' I got down and sat on a molehill by the chair. 'There must have been a bridge here. You'd think they'd've left it for cyclists and walkers, wouldn't you?'

Sam squinted upriver. 'No sign of it at all.' He slumped in his chair. 'Blast. I wanted to explore the whole length of the line.'

'Don't be daft, there must be another four or five miles of it.'

'How do you know?'

'Well, Lisa said it was ten miles long. It's about five miles into Kingscote from here, so another five must be all the way.'

'Suppose so.' He was definitely dejected. Or ill. My heart jumped uncomfortably. About twice every winter Sam was ill. Really ill. But it wasn't winter yet.

'You cold?' I asked casually.

'Nope.' He looked down at his hands. We hadn't bothered with gloves. He said slowly, 'Where does the train go from here?'

'What train?' I asked, still thinking about his hands.

'*Our* train, idiot! Is that why it drives through the house every night? Because it can't get through?'

I transferred my gaze to his face. He was serious.

'What on earth are you talking about?' I asked loudly. 'No train steams through our house – you know that perfectly well!'

He was surprised by my tone and looked up.

'Well . . . you know what I mean . . .' he said lamely.

I didn't. And neither did he.

'You'd better watch what you say!' I warned him roughly. 'You could be put in a funny farm for that kind of remark!'

He smiled right at me. 'Is it all right to say you

54

look like a garden gnome sitting on that little hill?'

I smiled back reluctantly. 'I suppose so. And it's not a little hill. It's a molehill.'

He laughed at that. ''Course it isn't a molehill. It's too big. It might be an old ant hill. Or—' His eyes sparkled again, 'Or buried treasure!'

That was the kind of fantasy I could go along with – just for his sake, of course.

I leapt up and pretended to go berserk.

'At last! At last! We've found it! After years of searching and finding maps and—'

He was spluttering with good, normal giggles. I was so relieved I gave the hillock a mighty kick then pretended I'd broken my foot. And as I hobbled around, hamming it up like crazy, Sam homed in on the decapitated hillock and pushed around with his cold fingers.

'Hey! Matt! Stop mucking about and come and look! There *is* something here!'

The soil was sandy and sticky at the same time. We both delved into it, still giggling and getting ourselves deliberately plastered. As Mum said later, I should have known better. I was so glad Sam was no longer in that other-world of his, I really didn't care about the mud.

There was material there. Cloth of some kind. I pulled and it tore away. I came up with a piece of something the size of a postage stamp.

'A body?' Sam suggested.

'Ha!' I waved the tiny shred in his face.

'Well, there might be more.' Sam plunged his hand in again and emerged with something firmer. It still felt like some kind of cloth but it was stiffer and there was more of it. We couldn't see what it was for mud, but I had a sudden nasty thought. Was it the peak of a cap? And was there a head to go with it? The blasted hillock would just about accommodate a human head.

'Well, that's it,' I said cheerfully. 'Chuck it away, Sam – probably full of germs. Let's get home.'

'Not yet. There might be something else . . .' He probed around with his fingers again and made a face. 'Can't feel a thing.'

'Listen, it's gone twelve and if we're not back for Sunday dinner, Mum will go spare.'

'Sunday dinner. Yuk,' Sam commented.

'All right, so it's not your fave. But Mum will still go spare if we—'

Sam suddenly slumped again. 'Yeah. OK. Wagons roll.'

But he didn't throw down the muddy hat brim . . . if that's what it was. He stuffed it down the side of his chair, which meant his trousers were going to be filthy.

I knew even then that I was going to get into trouble.

*   *   *

'You should have known better!'

But Mum's heart wasn't in it – she was too worried about Sam. He was soaking in a bath of water after refusing not only his Sunday roast, but apple pie as well.

'He's covered in mud and obviously exhausted. What possessed you to go so far? Did he fall out of his chair or something?'

'No, Ma. I've already told you. We wanted to find where the railway line went. And then when it ended we found this molehill and—'

'It's not Matt's fault, hon.' Dad and I were drying the dishes and he tried to put a comforting arm around Mum. The towel wrapped her face and she spluttered out of it. Dad went on soothingly. 'You know what Sam's like when he gets a bee in his bonnet. And he enjoys being with Matt so much he probably didn't realize himself he was getting tired and cold.'

'He never does, does he?' Mum said gloomily. I knew quite suddenly she was nearly crying. So did Dad because he put down the towel and enfolded her.

'I'll go and see he's all right,' I mumbled and made for the bathroom.

And he was. He looked back to normal, letting his useless legs float on top of the water and lying back like a Roman emperor. Except it looked more like a mud bath than anything with asses' milk or whatever they had in Roman times.

'I didn't realize you were so filthy!'

He grinned. 'Not only me.' He fished around under his bottom and produced something. 'It's this!' And he held aloft a crescent of stiffened serge. It was the part of the cap he had found. He'd washed it clean. It was navy blue, stitched firmly around the edge with something in its centre. A brooch? I thought of the molehill and felt queasy. *Was* there a head down there?'

He said, 'You know what it is, don't you?

'The peak of a cap, I'd say. Shall I run this water away and put in some fresh?'

'No. Mum always showers me when I'm on the seat.' He offered me the cap peak. 'You'd better take this. In case she blows her top.'

'Which she will.' I took the soggy lump from him and glanced at the brooch thing. And then I looked up and met his eyes which were fixed on me.

The brooch was a badge. We'd seen that badge before, Sam and me. It was worn by the men who worked at Temple Meads forty years ago and a lot of them still had them. The metal letters were contained in a circle and they were G and W and R. Great Western Railway.

Seven

Sam was ill for a week. The doctor came every day and talked about hospital, but after the last time Mum and Dad had promised Sam no more hospitals, so he stayed at home. He looked so small in Mum's big bed. He managed to talk and he could feed himself. But . . . he looked so small.

Dad slept in the bottom bunk. The strange thing was, during that week there were no midnight noises. None at all.

Everything except Sam seemed so – so petty and unnecessary. I even forgot about the possibility of a human head being buried in that ant hill along the sea wall. And school was just a waste of precious time: I told Hilda I wouldn't be able to make training on Saturday afternoon.

He looked down at me from his great height.

'What is it with you, Savernack? You've got potential. You can run and you're not afraid to tackle. But there's more to the game than that. There's . . . soul. Your soul's missing.'

I mumbled something.

He said, 'Sure nothing's up at home?'

'Sure.' I never told anyone about Sam. Don't

get me wrong, it wasn't shame. I didn't want him talked about.

'And you're not sick?'

'No.'

He clamped his mouth consideringly, then said, 'Be there. Saturday afternoon.' And he walked off.

I knew what that meant. If I didn't show up I was out of the team. I wanted to stay in rugger, but weekends were my only chance to be with Sam.

I skulked off to the end of the road where Dad always met me, and there was Jack Martin. It didn't matter too much; Sam wouldn't be in the car that night.

'Heard you getting a rollicking.' He grinned. 'We all know why you can't make Saturday.'

I stared at him. How on earth had anyone found out about Sam?

'It's a girl, isn't it? You've got a girlfriend!' Jack laughed like a lavatory flush and punched my shoulder. I realized suddenly I'd got the perfect excuse. I didn't say a word, just stuck a stupid half-grin on my face and rolled with his punches.

'You devil!' Jack was delighted. 'You've only been here five minutes . . . Who is she? Mandy Stephenson? Everyone goes out with Mand at least once in their first term.'

I just shook my head and kept grinning and wished Dad would arrive.

'Sally McPherson? Watch out for her dad, he's

an amateur boxer. Gemma Bridges? No! Don't tell me it's Caroline Roberts! I've seen her giving you her strip-stare! Lord, if it's Caroline—'

'It's not Caroline,' I said firmly. 'It's no-one from school.'

He came up with another list of names, presumably of local girls who went to the private school, and I knew that at any minute my damned face would give me away. And then, thankfully, the car drew up behind me.

It was Dad. Not only Dad, either. In the back seat, her face right against the window, was Lisa.

Jack said, awe-struck, 'Is that her?'

She was looking pretty awful. Red hair spiked up aggressively, brown eyes boring in on the two of us standing there on our legs with our hands holding school bags. She made you so conscious you'd got legs and hands, you didn't know what to do with them.

Dad leaned over and opened the door.

'Front or back, Matt?'

I met Lisa's challenging stare and just for a moment saw something I'd never noticed before and knew she expected me to choose the front seat.

I opened the rear door so that Jack could see her. She was wearing a long skirt and a long-sleeved blouse.

I said, 'I'll introduce you, Jack. Lisa, this is Jack Martin. Jack, this is my friend. Lisa.'

He was staring, almost open-mouthed, which

annoyed me a lot. I got in the car and slammed the door shut. Dad waved cheerfully enough and off we went.

Lisa said not a word. Dad told me he'd popped home at midday and Sam was on the mend and had asked if Lisa would come to tea. Then he asked me about school and I found things to say until we went over the old railway bridge and on to the moors. Then we were quiet, looking out at the big grey sky and the almost leafless hedges.

When we got Lisa's chair out and Dad had lifted her into it, she suddenly turned to me and grinned.

'What makes you think I'm your friend?' she asked.

I was taken aback. I'd thought she was so hurt by Jack's incredulity she'd been lost for words. I should have known better.

I stammered, 'Well . . . you're Sam's friend and so I thought . . .'

She pressed a button and her chair turned again and went up the ramp to the house.

'That's OK.' She spoke airily as if it didn't matter whether we were friends or not. Then she paused just inside the front door and added, 'I've known Jack Martin since we were kids. He's all right. Not much brain, but all right.'

I watched her go down the hall into Mum's bedroom. My mouth was open now.

★ ★ ★

Sam got up for tea and Mum put it on a round table in the conservatory and closed the door so we could run the train.

We watched a single engine go round the circuit a couple of times while we ate banana sandwiches. Lisa wore her false hand and managed better than Sam or me.

Sam said, 'I've told her about the cap.'

Lisa said, ' "Her"? Who's "her"? The cat's dinner?'

Sam said, 'Don't muck about. We want you to take it for your gramps to see.'

Sam had not consulted me about that decision but I did not question it. Lisa didn't either. I was ready to bet no-one else could get away with talking to her like that.

Sam said, 'The thing is, it's got the old GWR cap badge on the front. But our line – the Mushroom Line – was a private one, wasn't it?'

Lisa nodded slowly. And then looked at me.

'Just the cap, was it?' she asked.

Her mind was working like mine. Also – like me – she did not want Sam to know what she was thinking.'

'Yeah,' I said.

'Let's see it then.'

I switched off the train and opened the door. Mum came out of the kitchen and asked if we needed more cake, and I said yes and went into the bedroom for the cap brim which was still behind the radiator. It was so dry it was almost crisp. I stuffed it inside my sweater, picked up some mini choc rolls from Mum and closed the conservatory door again carefully.

Lisa was a long time looking at the segment of cloth with its metal badge dangling on one side. I knew she was searching for hairs or bits of skin or something.

'Sam washed it in the bath,' I told her.

'Right.' She put it in the bag which hung from her chair. Then turned to the table, 'There's a lot of cake here.'

'Start on this lot first. Mum thinks we've already eaten it.'

Lisa took a piece of Battenburg on to her plate, 'My fave,' she said, grinning at us like a monkey. 'Come on, Sam I'll race you through this.'

Sam tucked in. Without realizing it, he'd eaten almost as much as me. And it was down to Lisa.

Jack Martin was still awe-struck the next day.

'How did you do it?' he asked as I slung my books into my locker. 'She's got a tongue like a razor-blade! She's cut me down to size about fifty million times! How did you get to *know* her even?'

I did a quick re-think. Jack wasn't horrified by Lisa's disabilities. He was simply amazed that she had deigned to be my friend. I said, 'My fatal charm, of course.'

'I haven't noticed any fatal charm!' He didn't

even smile. 'But she was looking at you as if you had something— How did you meet her?'

'My dad is caretaker at Automobiles,' I said.

'Ah. Right.' He continued to look at me as if searching for that aforementioned charm. He obviously failed to find it and frowned. 'Listen, Matt. D'you know about Lisa?'

''Course I do, Idiot.'

'Not about that. No-one notices that any more. About her going to court so that she could stay with her grandfather. Conducting her own case. Badgering the local authority to let her do A levels here with us. You know she's coming here next year?'

I stared at him. 'No.'

'She's been in the Bristol paper – often. She lived with her mum at her grandad's house and when her mum went off with someone and later died, they wanted to put her in a residential home. She soon put a stop to that. And then she said Automobiles couldn't teach her anything once she was sixteen so she'd come here. She wants to go to university and read Political Science.'

'Good grief!'

'She's brainy.' He stared at me. 'I just can't understand what she sees in you!'

I was not about to tell him she put up with me because of my kid brother. So I smiled enigmatically. I think that's what it was.

Anyway, Jack must have tackled her about it because that evening she phoned me at home.

'How's Sam?' she opened.

'Not bad at all. He's up. Finished off those choc rolls for tea.' I wanted to tell her it was all her doing, but I didn't.

She said, 'I was hearing about rugby training.'

'Yeah? How?'

'That doesn't matter. I'll come over on Saturday. I've got a bit more info. From Gramps.'

'That's great.' I meant it.

'Yeah. Well then, you can do your training. It's better if Sam and I are by ourselves.'

'Oh.' I felt as if I'd just fallen down a flight of stairs. 'Oh. OK then.'

'Right. Bye.'

She put down the phone. I was an idiot to think for one moment she might have been coming over to see me as well as Sam.

Hilda was fiercer than ever on Saturday.

'Another twenty press-ups, Savernack. And faster, too!' he bawled as everyone got up to begin the run down to the beach. Then, as I passed him, already panting like Sam's shunter, he said, 'Put some of that sexual energy into your game, boy! It's not much to ask!'

Sexual energy indeed! I was getting some kind of a reputation for no good reason at all. But it sounded good and everyone grinned. I just hoped Lisa never got to hear about it.

Eight

'Lisa went to Bristol. To the newspaper offices.' Sam spoke almost accusingly. As if I should have thought of it a long time ago.

'What did she do? Skip school?' I tried not to sound sarcastic. 'And anyway, she told me she had some information from her gramps.'

'She said that so you wouldn't feel bad. He won't talk about the old railway at all. Lisa reckons he must have lost a friend in the crash.'

'Crash?'

'That's what she found out. She didn't skip school. She was doing a project about the ancient Egyptians and she needed to go to the museum. Dad took her.'

'And after that he also took her to the newspaper offices, did he?'

'Yes.'

'I thought it was supposed to be our secret?'

'She went to the newspaper offices to see if there was any reference to some old bits of stuff being brought to Bristol.' He spoke parrot-fashion. Lisa must have coached him or something.

'So she lied to Dad.' I don't know why, but I was beginning to dislike Lisa Jenkins.

Sam shook his head vigorously. ''Smatter of fact there was a report about an ancient tomb being ransacked just outside Cairo in eighteen . . . something. And just after, these old stones were given to the museum and when they were stuck together—'

'Yeah-yeah-yeah. A likely story. So what about this crash.'

'That was why they closed the Mushroom Line. Because of the crash. It would have taken too much money to build the bridge again, and anyway we were getting coal from Bristol and Avonmouth docks by then so—'

'Hang on!' I held up my hand. I was really angry with Lisa by this time. Sam had been ill – really ill – and here she was, filling his head with a jumble of facts about the ancient Egyptians and a railway crash and coal imports and whatever else she'd been yapping about all afternoon.

But he wasn't a bit bothered. He laughed and slapped at my raised hand like he does when Dad says, 'Give me five!'

'OK! I'll go more slowly. Lisa said you'd have difficulty taking it in!'

She did, did she? I said nothing. But I felt grim as I flopped into a chair by Sam and prepared to listen.

It seemed that the Mushroom Line had been financed by Sir Edward Kingscote back in the eighteen seventies; a narrow-gauge track for transporting coal wagons and the occasional passenger to and fro from the coal wharf twelve miles away. There had been a bridge over the Cote Stream where the old Romans had had their ferry – that was where Sam and I had walked that cold Sunday afternoon and where we had found the head – sorry, hat – buried. The whole thing was pretty homespun until well into the nineteen twenties when a signalling system based on the Great Western Railway's safety regulations was installed. The old GWR line ran parallel to the Mushroom Line, but twelve miles inland. They called it God's Wonderful Railway and they weren't too keen on the Mushroom Line.

Before the Second World War started in 1939, there were moves to close it on safety grounds. But then there was a shortage of coal everywhere and the Mushroom Line was given a reprieve. Three men were requisitioned from the Bristol engine shed to man the push-and-pull service and they operated it more or less successfully until December 1940.

It was one of the worse winters of the war. Coal was terribly short and the weather was bitter. The sea wall had not been built then and the tides often covered the track. Sometimes the train would steam through the water meadows with the sea lapping to the hubs of the open-spoke loco wheels. It acquired a reputation. It might be slow, but it always ran.

It was at this time that Bristol was taking a battering from the German Luftwaffe. In an effort to trick the reconnaissance planes, a series of bonfires were lit out on the moors. Several sticks of bombs were dropped each night for a week. Local farmers thought the craters were a small price to pay for the lives of their neighbours in Bristol. Whether the line was damaged at this time was anybody's guess.

The blizzards started on the twelfth of December. It meant a respite from the bombing raids and the three-man crew of the train made the most of it. They were running four trips every day in appalling weather conditions. On the eighteenth of December, the fourth trip left the wharf just before midnight. They must have been running blind. Even so, they should have seen the lanterns guarding the bridge. The safety procedure would have been for the guard to have walked forward to examine the track. No such thing happened. The train drew on to the bridge at midnight and the bridge collapsed. The three-man crew were never seen again.

During the Board of Trade inquiry which lasted only one day because by that time the bombing had started again, the mystery was compounded.

Old Gaffer Baker who ran sheep just clear of the water meadows by Cote Stream, had crossed the bridge earlier that evening to fetch a stray. He had actually heard the bridge creaking in the wind and had penned his sheep, got his bike and cycled into Little Kingscote Halt where the signalman lived in a railway cottage. There had been no-one there. He had left a note for the signalman and returned to the bridge to put storm lanterns in position to warn the train crew. He had gone back to the signalman's cottage; it was still empty.

He had crossed the bridge again just before dark and positioned more warning storm lanterns. To no avail. He had watched from his cottage window and seen the light from the engine start across the bridge, moving fast. The middle span collapsed into the stream ahead of the engine. The stream was a raging torrent at the time, but he had pulled a greatcoat over his nightshirt and searched the banks. It was hopeless. But when he went back to his bed, he looked out again and thought he saw a figure, almost glowing, mount a bicycle and ride along the track towards Kingscote. The chairman had asked him whether he had taken a drop of whisky to keep out the cold. He had said he never touched whisky, and cider did not affect him in any way. And that was that.

'The railway never ran again,' Sam concluded in a sepulchral voice.

'Well, it couldn't, could it?'

I didn't hold with Lisa Jenkins filling Sam's head with all this business. I thought I'd tell her so, too. It sounded to me as if she'd been deliberately trying to frighten him.

'Until we moved in,' Sam concluded, ignoring my interruption entirely.

'Don't start that again, for Pete's sake!'

'But it's true, Matt! And no-one else hears it 'cept us. You an' me. The Prices don't hear it. Dad didn't hear it when he slept in my bed. It's just for us.' He frowned. 'It's something to do with Grandad.'

'What *are* you talking about!'

'I just know it, Matt. Grandad is trying to tell us something.'

'For God's sake, Sam!'

'It's something good. I know that too.'

'I never heard such total rubbish in all my life!'

'Well. OK. OK then.' Sam looked hurt but also stubborn. 'I'm back in my own bed tonight. Let's just wait and see, shall we?'

You've guessed it. Whatever it was, shuddered through our room at midnight and took about three minutes to disappear into the distance. Only it wasn't three minutes. As usual, it was no time at all.

The next day it was raining buckets.

'I'm glad it's raining,' Mum said stoutly as Dad pulled faces at the sluicing windows. 'We couldn't have gone out anyway until Sam's chest is properly cleared up. We're not tempted now.' She smiled at us all. 'We'll make out our Christmas lists.'

Like I said, Mum adores making lists.

Dad protested. 'It's the absolute beginning of November!'

'Well, that's good. Give us time to change our minds,' she said.

Sam said, 'That means we'll need the catalogue.' He meant the model train catalogue. He always chose something for the trainset.

It was some time during the afternoon when he was having his rest that Lisa phoned.

'I want a word with you,' she said brusquely.

'I want a word with you too.' I refused to be intimidated by her. 'What have you been feeding my brother?'

'The truth.' She sounded surprised. 'I got it from newspaper reports. I just left bits out. Didn't make up a word of it—'

'He's got an imagination, you know. Mystery men with mystery bikes. He believes in ghost trains. Now it's ghost bikes!'

There was a silence then she said slowly, 'You're not very bright, Matt, are you? The man with the bike was the signalman. He saw it happen.'

'The signalman? What do you mean? Had he been there all the time? Did he know? What do you mean?'

I heard her sigh the other end. Then she said, 'Matt. The signalman was my grandfather. Whether he'd been there all the time – whether he knew the bridge was going to collapse . . . how should I know?'

I felt she'd punched me – yet again. I thought of that silent, introverted old man. Who, nevertheless, looked after his disabled granddaughter and did his best by her.

She asked sharply, 'Are you still there?'

'Yeah.' I breathed deeply. 'Lisa, I don't understand.'

She said quietly, 'Neither do I.'

'But you must have some idea?' What I meant was, she was so clever she must have formed some theory about the whole thing.

'The only idea I have is . . . is unacceptable,' she said. I heard her take a breath, then she blurted, 'I mean – he couldn't have deliberately arranged for that train to go over the edge, could he? Could he, Matt?'

I shook my head vigorously at the receiver. 'Well, of course not! He's not capable . . . and anyway, there would be no reason . . . no, that's just out!'

'They blamed him, you know.' She sounded suddenly warmer. She'd needed to be reassured about her gramps's innocence. 'That was in the paper, too. He was dismissed from the service. That was when he went into the army – he'd have gone anyway. But he never worked for the railway again. He lost his cottage. It must have been awful. Just awful.'

'No-one seems to know about it. I should have thought – in a small place like Kingscote—'

'It was just a paragraph in the paper. Don't forget the bombing was dreadful then. War news was the only kind anyone wanted to hear.'

'Yeah. Yeah. I can see that.'

'The thing is, Matt . . .' I heard her swallow. 'The thing is, he's ill. He had a sort of stroke last night. I had to ring the doctor. He was taken into the cottage hospital. He can't come home for a bit.'

I stared at the wall above the telephone. It was peach. Emulsion paint over the new plaster. Everything was so new and clean in the bungalow. It was ridiculous to think of ghost trains.

I said, 'What about you?'

'Oh, I'll be all right.' Her voice changed. It became hard and cheerful. 'I'm going to Thornbury Hall for a while. No big deal.'

Thornbury Hall was a residential school for the physically disabled. About twenty miles north of Bristol.

'But . . . Automobiles . . .'

'They'll have to manage without me for a couple of weeks.'

'But—'

'No big deal. I told you. I just wanted you to know. Tell Sam too.'

'But Lisa – how will we—? I mean if anything else crops up, how will we—?'

'There's a telephone there, you idiot! And I'll be cadging lifts to come and see Gramps!'

'But—'

'I think this is the hospital car. Yes it is. I'll have to go. Goodbye, Matt!'

She didn't wait for a reply. I was left holding the receiver, which hummed in my ear.

Nine

Jack wasted no time in getting me to himself in the playground the next day.

'Is it true?'

His eyes were pale blue and they rolled around like marbles in his eye sockets.

'What?'

'She told me they said it was getting too heavy and she'd have to be sent away.'

'What on earth are you talking about?' I'd had a bad night what with thinking of Lisa and her gramps and waiting for the train to go through the house.

'Come on, Matt. You know she's been taken away, do you?'

'Lisa? Yes.'

'Well. She told me it was because you and she . . . well, you know! The social workers thought it would be better if you were separated.'

'She told you that?'

'Yeah.'

I couldn't stop laughing. And feeling . . . sort of . . . chuffed. Trust Lisa to go out on a joke.

'You didn't hear that her gramps was in the cottage hospital?'

'No.'

'Well, he is. So she couldn't stay in the house on her own, could she?'

Jack exploded. 'That girl! She's got everyone on a bit of string! Just because she's got no hands or feet we think she's some kind of saint!'

I went on laughing. 'She's not that,' I said.

Jack grinned unwillingly. And then said the most amazing thing I'd heard for a long time.

'Trouble is, she's so pretty!'

I had French and he had History so we parted then. I thought about Lisa. Pretty, she was not. But I knew what he meant. She did have something once you'd got used to the spiked hair. And he was right about one thing. She had everyone on a string.

But yesterday, on the phone – she hadn't been stringing me along then. Lisa Jenkins had let me see her properly once or twice. It was only because of Sam – I knew that. But it was pretty good all the same.

When Dad met me, we went to the hospital and sat by Mr Jenkins's bed for ten minutes. He wasn't saying much but he didn't look too bad and when he did speak you could understand every word.

'He's going to be fine,' the nurse said as she took his temperature and held his wrist.

'Home in a couple of weeks, I wouldn't be surprised.'

I thought that meant Lisa would be back too,

but Dad shook his head when I mentioned it in the car.

'I shouldn't think so, Matt. He won't be able to look after himself very well, let alone Lisa.'

My heart fell several centimetres in my chest cavity. Yeah, I know that's impossible but it happened.

The rest of that month went by practically without incident, which just went to show how Lisa stirred things up.

The only thing was, Sam did not go back to Automobiles. He hardly ever coughed but the doctor said that being quiet at home was the best thing for him. Mr Barker came to see him and brought some worksheets and on Bonfire Night we took him to see the fireworks in his school playground. He loved that and scooted around in his chair like a maniac with the other kids. And he came to see me in my first match for the Comp. It was against a team from Avonmouth who all looked as if they might have been three metres tall and then someone had hammered them down to shorter than most of us and their shoulders and thighs had taken up the extra mass. They had the squat, powerful bodies respected by all rugby players. I was suddenly thankful that Hilda had driven us so hard during our training sessions.

We lost, but respectably, and Sam yelled from the sidelines louder than anyone. In the dressing-room Hilda said that for a side of undernourished, lily-livered, brainless twits, we hadn't done too badly. We glowed.

That night, after Sam was in bed and Mum and Dad were watching a film made in 1935, I telephoned Thornbury.

'Right.' Lisa said immediately she picked up the phone. 'Did you win?'

'How did you know it was me? It could have been anyone!'

'No-one else phones on Saturday nights. Did you win?'

'No.'

'Blast. Did you score?'

'I got a touchdown. They were massive blokes but not that good at running.'

She said with a kind of yearning, 'You've got good running legs.'

And, without thinking, I blurted, 'You know I'd give them to you if I could!'

I could have bitten out my tongue. It was the kind of stupid remark Lisa hates, and in any case, did I mean it? Could I bear to be in a chair like her and Sam?

She was silent for so long I knew she was preparing to cut me down to size.

Then there was a sound like an explosion on the line as she cleared her throat and she said, 'I wasn't going to tell you. They reckon – in time – I could use artificial legs. Like that pilot, Douglas Bader, did in the Second World War.'

'*Lisa!*'

'I don't like the thought of stumping along so – so ungracefully.' She forced a little laugh. 'I'm terribly vain you know, Matt.'

I too managed a laugh. 'I know,' I came back.

She spluttered with real laughter. 'You – you *swine*!'

'Yeah.'

She stopped laughing and said briskly, 'What news of Gramps?'

I gave her an update. He'd sort of levelled out and wasn't making more progress. He looked pretty frail. I told her the truth.

She said, 'I'm coming in to see him again on Monday. I want you to do something for me.'

'I'll meet you at the hospital—'

'No. Don't skip school. But you can go to see him on Monday night?'

'Yeah. Any time.'

'Make it Monday night. Strike while the iron's hot.'

'What? Why? How?'

'Shut up a minute. This is difficult so I'll just say it. OK?'

'You always do.'

'I'm not mucking about now, Matt.' I heard her take a deep breath. 'I don't think Gramps will be going home again.'

'Total balderdash. He's only seventy-five. That's nothing these days—'

'And he's got something on his mind. He can't tell me. But he needs to tell someone before he can die. I think he might tell you.'

I was shocked into temporary silence and she said, 'I know it's a lot to ask—'

I said, 'Look. For one thing, he's not going to die. For another, we know what he's got on his mind – he had to take the rap for his mates being killed and then the railway being closed— And why should he tell me? I'm a stranger and—'

'That's why he'll tell you. If he'll tell anyone. But don't push him – he's very stubborn and if he thinks you and me have cooked anything up—'

'I don't think I'm the right one – get him to tell you, for Pete's sake—'

'I'll try, of course. But he's got this thing about burdening me – treats me as if I'm made of glass—'

'Ha!'

'Quite. So you'll go on Monday night and just let him talk – if he will.'

'I suppose so.'

'Good. Bye.'

And she was gone.

Mum said behind me, 'I'm making cocoa. D'you want some.'

'Yes please.' I was as dry as a bone.

'Lisa all right?'

'Yeah. Top form. As usual.'

Mum poured milk into a pan. 'I wish Sam was as tough as she is. When I asked her if she'd come to tea, she said she was making a new life for herself and wanted to be left alone for a bit.'

'Did she?' I knew she wanted to be left alone to work out the business about her gramps. To come to terms with . . . whatever had happened all those years ago; to face the prospect that he might not live very much longer.

And then that night something happened that shoved everything else to the back of my mind.

I would have slept through the noise of our ghost train passing through the house – every bone in my body was aching – but Sam pulled on the dressing-gown cord and woke me just after the rumble had left our room.

'Wossup?' I asked blearily. ''Sonly the train—' Even I was calling it a train now.

Sam hissed, 'Something else! Listen!'

I listened, trying to separate the train rumble from . . . what? There was something. Another rumble.

Sam's hiss was tensile with excitement. 'It's the train!'

'I know that—'

'Our train! Gramps's train! The layout! It's working by itself!'

'Imposs!' But I was already swinging to the floor. It was our trainset and as it was definitely impossible for it to work itself, there was someone in the conservatory.

I whipped through the bedroom door, shouting for Dad as Sam was struggling into his chair, and was down the hall to the glass doors at the end in about two seconds. In fact, just as our other train – the ghost train – left Little Kingscote Halt and started on the curve of the coast which put it out of earshot. No sound from Dad's room.

The moonlight was strong that night – it was going to be a frost for the first of December. The conservatory was lit eerily but quite clearly. No-one was inside. But there, chugging around the track with a kind of persistent stoicism, was our small banker drawing about six coal wagons and a brake van.

I stood by the door, looking through, and waited for Sam and Dad to join me. It was terribly cold. The heating goes off in the night. Sam arrived and we both began to shiver.

After watching a complete circuit. Sam whispered, 'It's not imposs.'

'Yes it is. Something's happened to trip the switch. Dad must have set the heating to go on and—'

'Don't be daft!'

'Well, we'll ask him. Where on earth is he?'

'Matt . . .' Sam sounded pitying. 'It's the special time. Dad's not coming.'

I didn't argue. Just opened the conservatory door which meant the circuit was automatically broken. The bank engine could not move until the door was closed again and the circuit reconnected. Except that it did. I opened the door just after it had drawn clear, and it continued to chug around a loop line, disappear into a tunnel and was just re-emerging when Sam joined me.

We took up positions in the centre of the floor and continued to stare.

The banker was going slowly as if up a real bank. The small pellets we used to make smoke were working overtime, and it was belching thick smoke from its squat funnel and obviously labouring. It rounded the curve and began on the straight that led to the gap where the door was still open.

Suddenly Sam moved. He pushed himself towards the small ground frame situated just this side of the door and flicked it. The signal clicked into the 'off' position.

'What do you think you're doing?' I whispered. 'There's no-one on the blooming thing!'

The banker reached the signal which was glowing red in the moonlight and passed it.

'You see?' Sam hissed triumphantly. 'It passed the signal at Danger!'

'But there's no-one *on* it!' I repeated furiously.

I got no further because the banker had reached the gap in the line where the door was still open. Slowly, deliberately, it drove itself over the edge, dragging its load behind it all anyhow. It hit the carpet with a muffled thud and suddenly the conservatory was silent. Terribly, horribly, silent.

Ten

Sam and I were in a state of shock all day Sunday. I dreaded going to bed that night. But nothing happened. I didn't sleep much though and I don't think Sam did.

There were two wards in the cottage hospital: on the left of the reception desk were the women, on the right were the men. The signs were clear and large but they did not say which way you had to be facing when you worked the whole thing out, so naturally I managed to get into the women's ward. When I asked for Mr Jenkins I was escorted back to the foyer as if I intended to rape everyone there.

She pointed to the signs.

'Yes, I know. But if you face the door, *this* is your right—'

She manhandled me to the door labelled 'Men' and opened it for me, soliloquizing about the youth of today as she did so. I could have told her I was half-asleep because I'd been waiting for a ghost train all night, but it didn't seem appropriate.

The men's ward had a very high arched ceiling, churchy windows and a vinyl floor that looked like a virgin ice rink but was strangely tacky beneath my trainers. There were ten beds along one wall and ten beds along the other. At the end of the ward was a table where most of the beds' occupants were gathered. So it was easy to find Gramps. I managed to wedge a chair by his locker and get myself into it without too much fuss. Even so, a hush fell on the ward and everyone looked.

'Hello, Mr Jenkins,' I said heartily. 'It's me, Matthew Savernack. From Little Kings—'

'I remember you,' he replied sourly. 'No need to shout, I'm not deaf. And watch you don't knock that lemonade bottle over.'

He was sliding down his back-rest thing, looking as taciturn as he'd looked when he brought Lisa to see us or collected her from Automobiles. I hardly knew the bloke. What on earth Lisa expected, I did not know.

Picking up my thoughts practically uncannily, he said, 'You just missed her.'

'Who?' I knew darned well who.

'Lisa. She said you'd be in.' He spoke without any pleasure at all. 'Reckons you're still missing your own gramps.'

'Yeah?' I cleared my throat loudly. This was embarrassing.

'She's got the idea me and 'im were something like. Both a bit mad when it comes to trains.'

I had to put a stop to this. I trumpeted an enormous cough and gasped, 'How is she?'

He opened his eyes properly and looked at me for the first time.

'All right. She's all right. Best thing that could have happened to her, me having this stroke.'

I spoke heartily again. 'She wouldn't agree with you there, Mr Jenkins!'

'Because she's a sentimental female. But I know what I know. She'll be all right at Thornbury. Get all those letters she needs to go to university.' His eyes drooped and he slid further down his back-rest. 'She's going to be Prime Minister one day. Did you know that?'

I hooted a genuine laugh. 'No! I did not!'

'Well, she is.' He opened his eyes and dug his elbows into his pillows. 'Just you remember that, boy! D'you hear me?'

The gaggle of dressing gowns at the end of the ward were listening hard. I said quickly, 'Yeah. Sure. I reckon Lisa could be anything she wanted.'

'That's a fact. And don't you forget it!'

He began to slip again and I half stood to help him up on to the rest, but he moved his head in negation.

'Just leave her alone, boy. Don't get in the way.'

'Mr Jenkins – I wouldn't – I don't know what you mean—'

'You know what I mean, boy. She's all right where she is. And she'll be free. She can forget me and all my troubles and that's the way I want it!'

Lisa had put her foot in it somewhere. Mr Jenkins

was not going to tell me a thing.

But I had to try.

I stayed leaning over him so that the dressing gowns couldn't hear what I said.

'Maybe she could put it all behind her if she knew . . .' He opened one evil eye and stared at me. '. . . the truth,' I concluded lamely.

We stared at each other for what seemed an age. His eye had a slight wobble, but it was focused well and truly on me and I had to force myself to meet it.

Then, just as I thought I must fall on top of him through sheer exhaustion, he whispered, 'Well . . . you can tell her I'm not a murderer.'

I took a breath.

'As if she would—'

'Tell her I'm not a murderer. But I could have been. And I thought I was. And so did everyone else.'

The dressing gowns were very quiet.

'Tell her, if she needs proof then—'

The elderly Sister spoke from the region of my shoulder and I leapt up, hitting her jaw with my head so that she shrieked with pain. I turned in mid-leap to catch her as if she were a rugby ball and sort of waltzed with her towards the dressing gowns.

It was total chaos. I don't even like to think of it now. In the nick of time Dad appeared at the door of the ward saying, 'What on earth—?' and all I could say was, 'I jumped and hit her jaw with my head and—'

'He attacked me!' she yelped, collapsing over the table and scattering dominoes on to the floor.

Dad said resignedly, 'He's a rugby player, you see . . .'

And behind us a strange noise overtook the rest of the bedlam.

Mr Jenkins was laughing.

Luckily, Dad was so full of the hilarious scene he'd found in the men's ward of the cottage hospital, it did not occur to anyone to ask what Mr Jenkins and I had talked about. The thought of me knocking the Sister cold tickled Sam to death. He'd been looking rather big-eyed when I got home that Monday night and I was glad he could find something to laugh about. So I re-enacted it all several times, getting dafter each time until Mum said we were both hysterical and the sooner we got a good night's sleep the better.

She was right and we knew it. We almost forgot to connect the dressing-gown telephone cord and I reckon we were asleep within five minutes of putting the lights out. But then, at five to twelve, we were awake. In unison. No need for anyone to pull the cord. It was as if we were conditioned to wake up in time for the train.

Sam whispered, 'It's late.'

'No.' I looked at the luminous hands on my watch. 'Five minutes to go.'

There was a silence in the dark room. Then Sam breathed, 'It never stops, does it?'

I'd given up scoffing. I whispered, 'No.'

'Yet Little Kingscote was a proper halt. People got on and off.'

'It was a request halt.' I tried to laugh. 'Presumably no-one wants to get off here any more.'

'A request halt,' Sam murmured.

'Yeah. You ask the guard if the train will stop—'

'I know. I know. I hadn't thought of it before.'

'So what?'

'So nobody has asked the guard to stop.'

I didn't reply. Who would be on our ghost train, anyway?

The rumble started in the distance and as it drew nearer, Sam whispered something else.

'What?' I asked.

'Yet,' he replied.

And for some reason I felt suddenly very afraid.

Sam was asleep before five past twelve. But I stayed awake for some time that night. Was there someone on that train who might want to get off at Little Kingscote Halt one day? And how was that connected to Lisa's gramps? Had he accidentally killed someone? And were they looking for him?

Eleven

The rest of that week stumbled by. We trained after school on Wednesday night: we were playing Almondsbury Comp. on Saturday. Away. Every night Sam and I woke at five to twelve, listened till the train went through, then fell asleep again. It's amazing how soon extraordinary happenings become ordinary. If it hadn't been for a heavy dread in the pit of my stomach, I could have accepted the ghost train as one of those things.

When Dad and I arrived home on Friday, the doc was still there giving Sam the once-over.

'Your mother has asked me to examine you too, Matt.' He was a nice-enough chap but I associated doctors with Sam being ill. 'She says you're under par.'

'I'm fine.' I gave Mum a look that should have dropped her in her tracks. She smiled lovingly at me. 'Bit tired.'

'Sam tells me you're not getting good nights.'

What had Sam been saying? We'd both end up in the funny farm if we weren't very careful indeed.

'Nothing to worry about. We get our ten hours.'

I spoke bitterly. Most boys of fourteen are allowed to stay up till midnight. Not me.

'You're doing a lot of physical exercise . . .' He had his ears plugged with his stethoscope so there was no need for more conversation. He sounded my front and back, looked down my throat, into my eye sockets, ears and – I'm almost certain – nostrils.

'Fine!' He straightened, smiling professionally. 'Very fit. Nothing to worry about.'

'I haven't been worried,' I said.

'Break up for Christmas soon, do you?' He was packing his stuff away, ignoring my sarcastic tone entirely.

'Ten days,' I muttered, buttoning my shirt angrily.

'Then enjoy it.' He straightened, looked at Sam then me and repeated, 'Enjoy it. That's an order.'

Mum said, 'Would you like a cup of tea, doctor?'

'No thanks. I'm calling at the Price farm.'

Mum led the way out, asking if anything was wrong with the Prices.

I said to Sam, 'What did he mean by that? How can you order anyone to enjoy Christmas?'

Sam shrugged.

I pulled my head through my sweatshirt.

'And what happened to ye olde family doctor who stopped for a cup of tea and a chat?'

Sam shrugged again.

Then, as the front door closed, 'I told him about the train.'

I was aghast. 'You what?'

'I told him it never stops. He said we didn't want it to stop. Not for another seventy years. What did he mean, Matt?'

I clutched my head. 'He thinks we're mad! He'll have a chat with the psychiatrist—'

'I didn't say *you* heard it. Only me.' Sam grinned. 'He'll think I'm a fanciful child!'

Sam couldn't come to the match. He had another cough. It was quite a long drive in the coach and there'd been a frost the night before, which meant that the Gloucestershire hedges were rimed with silver like a Christmas card. It also meant the pitch was going to be like iron. It was. We lost. Which was a great pity because I spotted Lisa's wheelchair at half-time. She was in the midst of a knot of parents and other 'fans'. She wore a long plaid skirt and a cape with a hood. She reminded me of a Victorian character. All muffled and mysterious.

They had a nice clubhouse at Almondsbury and she was waiting there at a table with two glasses of something and a plate of sandwiches.

'Thought you might be hungry. Did you hear me cheering?'

'I think so.'

'Didn't do much good, did it? Thought you said you could run?'

'I did. I can. On decent ground. It's like running on ice today.'

'Didn't stop that other kid, did it? You've been skipping training.'

'I have not!'

'Well then, you haven't put your heart into it.'

'I've had a lot on my mind.'

'Like what? Telephoning me perhaps?'

'There was nothing to say.' I practically choked on a sandwich and stopped to chew it a bit more.

She said thoughtfully, 'Gramps told you something. I know that much. Otherwise you would have telephoned. But then he said I was going to be Prime Minister and should be left to get as many exams as possible.'

I managed a sarcastic, 'Ha!'

'But I'll need supporters. In my inner Cabinet.'

I blinked and stared at her. She was grinning like a monkey.

'All right,' she said. 'Let's hear it. What did he say?'

There were people milling around. Jack Martin was trying to get away from the rest of the side and join us.

I said, 'Now is not the time or the place, Lisa. You've come to see us play rugby.'

It was her turn. 'Ha!' she said.

'Well, why did you come then?'

'Thornbury is two miles away. Easy to cadge a lift. And I need to know about Gramps, Matt.' She leaned forward. 'I have to know!'

Jack Martin fought his way through everyone and said, 'Hi, Lisa. How's it going?'

She smiled at him blindingly. 'Splendidly, Jack! Thornbury is like a four-star hotel! And today – the match – so very exciting!'

Jack didn't even realize she was being sarcastic. He simpered sickeningly.

She handed him her glass. 'Could you possibly get me a cup of tea, Jack? This orangeade tastes of petrol.'

The inference was that I'd bought the orangeade and laced it accordingly. Jack gave me a triumphant look. 'Be right back.'

She hissed, 'And he will too! What did Gramps say?'

'He said he wasn't a murderer. And if you needed proof . . .'

'Yes? If I needed proof?'

'I don't know. I knocked the Sister's head off then and he was laughing so much he couldn't tell me.'

The look she gave me was . . . withering.

Jack said, 'I remembered you don't take sugar, Lisa. And I brought you a cake.'

Lisa looked at the tea, then back at Jack.

She said, 'Sorry, Jack. I've changed. I do take sugar now. Could you possibly . . .'

He was gone and she said, 'Proof of what, Matt?'

I looked down and said, 'Proof that he wasn't a murderer. He said he wasn't a murderer, Lisa.'

She turned on me. 'And you didn't think that was important enough to tell me on the phone?' When I did not reply she went on furiously, 'I never thought he *was* a murderer, anyway! Did you?'

'Of course not. But there could have been some kind of horrendous accident—'

'And you think there was a body underneath that cap? Have you dug further down?'

'Of course not! Sam might think it rather odd if I went off without him, carrying a spade!'

She checked her anger and sat back slightly. 'Sam. How is Sam?'

'OK now. I think. But he told the doctor about the ghost train. And there's something else you don't know. Last Saturday the train layout started working—'

Jack said, 'Here's the sugar bowl, Lis. How many spoonfuls?'

She glanced at him absently. 'Four.'

He ladled and stirred industriously.

I said suddenly, 'Where did your grandfather used to live, Lisa? Before he moved into Kingscote?'

She picked up her cup and sipped, then pulled a terrible face.

Jack said, 'Isn't it OK? I'll get you another—'

She spluttered, 'It's fine. Fine.'

'Try the cake.'

She bit obediently.

I repeated, 'Where did he actually live?'

Jack said, 'Shut up, Sav. Can't you see she's eating?

Someone bawled, 'Three cheers for Kingscote! Hip hip—'

Lisa said, 'There was a railway cottage. At the Halt. Probably where your bungalow is now.'

'HOORAY!'

I said. 'Oh no! He lived at Little Kingscote Halt?'

'He was in charge of the Halt, remember.'

'For Pete's sake, Lisa!'

'What?'

The Almondsbury captain was lifted on to one of the tables.

'For he's a jolly good fellow . . .' everyone was singing, even our lot. The Almondsbury side had been good.

I leaned towards her. 'Because if he did kill someone accidentally, they might come for him. They might stop at the Halt.'

'What on earth are you talking about?'

She'd been in a normal environment too long. She didn't understand any more.

I said, 'I think the coach is ready now. It was nice to see you, Lisa. Jack – come on!'

He said, 'Hang on – I haven't had a chance to ask Lisa—'

Her face was bright red. 'You needn't bother to ring! If you really think that about my Gramps—'

I said, 'I told you – I never thought—'

Jack said, 'Is he all right? The old man?'

Lisa said, 'Why don't you jump off a cliff, Jack?'

He flushed suddenly. 'I only asked— Anyone would think I'd done a murder or something!'

She whirled away and by the time we got on to the coach there was no sign of a plaid skirt anywhere.

Jack was still aggrieved. 'What's with her?' he grumbled. 'We used to be good mates and now she snaps my head off—'

'Worried about her grandfather.'

He thought about it then said grudgingly, 'I suppose she talks to you because your grandfather lived with you.'

I nodded. 'He bought a railway line once. It must have been just like the Mushroom Line.'

'The Mushroom Line?'

'Oh . . . that's another story,' I said. And was glad when Hilda started everyone singing.

Twelve

That evening the cold intensified and a wind from Siberia started to blow over the Somerset Levels. Dad put the heating on high, smiling with satisfaction – the tall house in Bristol had never been really warm.

It must have been the cold that tightened my muscles. I couldn't get comfortable in any of the chairs and was stupid enough to let out a groan every now and then.

Mum acted as if I was Sam's age. 'I don't care what the doctor said. You look terrible. I think you should have some aspirin and go straight to bed.'

'I'm stiff. That's all. That ground was as hard as—'

'A good night's sleep is what you need then,' Mum argued inexorably. 'And you know an aspirin always works wonders with you.'

In the end I had an aspirin and went to bed just to stop her. But I didn't want to sleep. My 'chat' with Lisa had done me no good at all. Somehow I was now convinced that because her gramps had something to do with that train crash all those years ago, the men who had died in it were trying to come back for him. I had to stay awake in case the train stopped at Little Kingscote Halt.

It did not stop that night. The wind was howling so hard that even the rumbling sounds coming up the bunk posts were barely felt. I breathed deeply and pushed my head into my pillow and let sleep take over. A second later, Sam pulled on our communication cord.

'Wossup?' I asked blearily, trying to fight off the aspirin effects all over again.

Sam was already half out of bed.

'Come on. It's the trainset.'

Somehow I fell down the ladder and stumbled after the wheelchair. The wind sounded like wolves outside. Sam must have ears like Mr Spock's to hear the trainset above that.

But he was right. By the time we'd got the conservatory door open, our eyes were used to the darkness and we could see the banker with its load of coal wagons just entering the tunnel facing us.

I closed the door and stood in the middle of the room like a zombie, turning my body slowly to watch the train go round. Sam shoved his chair back to the door and moved the signals to red. The train sailed past them and went on chugging through the first of Grandad's stations, then the goods yard, then the tunnel, then the second station. Just before it reached the door, Sam bowled across and pulled on the handle. The line was cut . . . just as surely as it had been cut in 1940 when the bridge had collapsed into the Cote Stream. Once again the banker ignored the fact that the electrical circuits had been broken and continued to the brink and then over and on to the carpet.

I continued to stare helplessly while Sam leaned over and shovelled the train on to his lap and then set it up again the other side of the door.

Immediately it was assembled, the blasted thing started up again. The first station, the goods yard, the tunnel . . . and then, before the second station, Sam wheeled himself quickly to the ground frame there and adjusted the points so that the banker would take its load into one of the sidings.

The little engine jerked slightly as it reached the points, then it went straight over them still on the main line, continued through the station, up to the open door and, again, crashed to the ground.

Sam bowled across to the ground frame, stared closely at it, fiddled a bit, then looked at me.

'The points were reset for the main line,' he whispered.

'You couldn't have changed them properly – I noticed the engine juddered a bit—'

Sam breathed, 'OK. We'll do it again. Put the stock back on the line.'

I leaned down, picked up the train and began to place it carefully on the line. It started immediately. I whipped over to Sam and checked that the points at the second station were set for the siding. As I did so, I realized my muscles were no longer aching.

The train approached the station, reached the junction, juddered as before then continued along the main line and crashed to the floor. We both peered down at the tiny ground frame. The points were set for the main line. Yet I knew that this time they had been set for the siding.

Sam said, 'It's trying to tell us something, Matt. What is it?'

Wearily, I picked up the train.

'I don't know. How do we stop the wretched thing?'

'What's the time?' Sam asked irrelevantly.

I glanced at my watch. 'About half a minute past midnight.'

Sam said, 'It won't go again. The time freeze is over.'

And my muscles were screaming too. I put the train on the track clumsily. Nothing happened.

'I've got to get to bed, Sam. Come on.'

Sam trundled ahead of me. The wind howled. I got him into his bunk, tucked him in and put a blanket over his duvet. I did the same for myself. The very next instant Mum's voice said, 'You've slept really late, Matt. Have a cup of tea and tell me how you feel.'

It was gone ten by my watch. The wind had dropped. Mum had pulled the curtains and the lane leading to the Price farm looked scoured and raw.

I said, 'Oh, Mum. It's great to be here.'

I don't know why I said it. Mum smiled at me and risked a peck at my forehead. And I sat up and drank my tea and listened to Sam singing in the bathroom and wondered what we were supposed to do about living on this busy railway junction.

Neither of us was allowed out, but Dad went down for the milk and told us that Mr Price had flu but the doc had left him some antibiotics and he was already better. I wondered if I'd got it too and last night had been an hallucination. But I knew it wasn't.

After Sunday dinner, Mum and Dad went for a lie-down while we watched *Blackbeard the Pirate*. Sam waited for their bedroom door to close then switched off and said, 'We should talk about the train. Why does it go by itself? Why does it keep going over the edge whatever we do to stop it? What is it trying to tell us?'

'It's happened twice, that's all. And how could a train be trying to tell us anything?' I didn't want to think about it. I wanted to watch *Blackbeard* and pretend I was a normal kid.

He said fretfully, 'I wish Lisa hadn't gone away. She'd believe me.'

'Matter of fact, she was at the match yesterday. She didn't believe *me*.'

'You told her? About the layout working by itself?'

'Yeah.'

'And she didn't believe you?'

'Well, she didn't exactly disbelieve me . . . she just didn't take much notice of me.'

He was impatient. 'That's just her. Pretending not to care. You're such an idiot, Matt!'

Before I could think up a return insult, the phone rang and I snatched at it before it woke up Mum and Dad.

It was her.

'Listen. I've got two things I want you to do.'

'Only two?'

'The first is to get along the sea wall where you found the cap and dig deeper. You know why.'

'Lisa. I explained to you why that was impossible. And now . . . the ground is hard as iron and I've got flu.'

'Poor baby. The second is, when you find there's nothing there, I want you to go back and find out what Gramps has in the way of proof.'

'And if there is something there?' The thought of it made me queasy. What would be there after fifty-three years? Bones? Teeth? Oh help.

'Then you go and talk to Gramps to find out what he has in the way of—'

'Yeah. Yeah. Yeah. So you need proof?'

'Not for myself, idiot. Of course I know Gramps isn't a murderer. He couldn't hurt a fly. Literally. He won't have any aerosols or even fly-papers—'

'No-one else remembers that night anyway, so why dig it all up again.'

'You are so thick. I can't believe you. For *his* sake, of course! He needs to know that we know that—'

'Lisa. I'm sorry but—'

'Is Sam there?'

'Yeah.'

'Let me just wish him a happy Christmas then.'

I handed the receiver over wearily. Sam was grinning. He said 'Hi,' and then, 'Not bad,' and then he listened. His grin disappeared. Then he said, 'That's what the train is trying to tell us, Lisa! It's trying to tell us that whatever your gramps had done that night, it had to go over!'

He looked over the handset at me. 'I thought you said she didn't believe you? She's been thinking a lot about it and—'

I took the phone from him. 'Lisa. Please. I'll do what you say, but just let us watch *Blackbeard*. OK?'

The phone went dead.

Sam said, 'Listen, Matt. Stop worrying about me. It's you who is getting into a state about all this. It's not worrying me – I'm enjoying it! It's better than *Blackbeard* or going to Automobiles or anything! You should have told me what you and Lisa were thinking. Lisa said I've got a clear head. Well, perhaps I have because it's as plain as your face to me – that night the train was going to go over that bridge and into the river whatever happened. Nothing – no-one – could stop it. Don't you see?'

'No.' I put the receiver back carefully. I was so tired and Lisa had put an end to our quiet afternoon.

Sam said patiently, 'Our layout has only worked by itself in December. Yes?'

'I suppose so.'

'Well, it has. Think about it. Both times Saturdays. Both in December.'

'So?'

'The real train crash happened in December, on a Saturday, in a blizzard.'

'Good grief.' I put my head in my hands.

'Nothing we can do will stop our banker going over the edge of the rail where the door breaks the circuit.'

I said nothing.

'And nothing would have stopped that train going on to the bridge and crashing into the river,' Sam concluded.

I sighed. 'So what does that prove?'

'Listen, Matt.' Sam bowled his chair up to my knees and tried to talk into my face. 'Lisa's gramps must have been there. Trying to stop the train. It must have been him the farmer saw – with the bike. He had to watch the whole thing happen. Three men – his friends – were killed. And he couldn't do anything.'

I said dully, 'He was the wrong side of the river.'

'What?'

'If he'd examined the bridge he would have seen what the farmer saw. And he could then have gone over to the other side and stopped the train with his red lamp. But he was seen this side of the river.'

Sam said obstinately, 'Perhaps that's why he blames himself. But we know – the train is telling us – there is an explanation. And we've got to find it.' He sat back and drew a breath. 'You've got to go and dig up that ant hill, Matt.'

I put my hands on my knees and stared at him. 'She told you that?'

'And you've got to go now. Before Mum and Dad wake up.'

'Sam! Every bone in my body—'

'Then you can go to see Lisa's gramps tomorrow after school.'

'Sam – the ground will be—'

'Take the fork as well as the spade. And you can borrow my Balaclava.' Sam had a hideous knitted helmet which made him look like a bank robber. I wouldn't be seen dead in it.

Five minutes later I was walking along the sea wall, shouldering the fork one side, the spade the other, and wearing Sam's Balaclava.

Thirteen

Like I said, the wind had gone and the countryside looked as if someone had been at it with a
Brillo pad. Out in the Channel, Steep Holme and
Flat Holme appeared to be licking their wounds.
The sky was grey, low and gentle. Halfway along
the wall I looked back; the bungalow had disappeared from view but I could see Prices' Farm
and smoke curling up from their chimney. The
gulls were silent; a skein of geese flew overhead
and honked. Otherwise, nothing.

Without Sam's wheelchair I walked to the river
in fifteen minutes. I felt better. Soothed by the
emptiness perhaps. Below me, the depression in
the flood meadows showed where the train had
trundled fifty-three years before. Without the hump
of the sea wall to obscure the view, it must have been
a beautiful run. I half closed my eyes and tried to
imagine it. Very peaceful. Except in a storm.

I reached the muddy waters of the Cote. The
banks were steep and slimy, protected now by a
fence. But then . . . it must have been a terrify-
ing sight. Had the train dropped clear like it did
back in the conservatory? Or had it slithered down

that steep incline like a huge unwieldy toboggan?

I thought of Lisa's gramps lying in his hospital bed, and I shuddered. He hadn't murdered anyone – I knew that as well as Lisa. But he had seen it happen; he had been unable to do anything to stop it. Maybe he had found a body and buried it. Whatever had happened, the inquiry had held him responsible. Responsible for the deaths of three men.

I didn't know why I was doing this. At that moment I nearly turned and went back home. But then I looked at the ant hill, decapitated just before Sam had been so ill. It looked . . . odd. I decided I would dig it flat. Whether it was a grave or not, it must be allowed now to melt into the flat landscape.

The strange thing was, it was so easy. The soil was sandy and had been held together by the mat of couch grass which we had sliced off. I stuck the fork into the side very, very gingerly and lifted. The soil ran through the tines like sugar or salt. There was absolutely nothing there to stop it. No bones, hair . . . nothing.

I tried again, deeper this time, and came up with nothing. And then, emboldened, and also amazed that my poor muscles were allowing me to do this, I took the spade and began to slice the surrounding turf. Half an hour later I had a depression which measured what seemed to me like the size of a grave. It wasn't deep – barely half a metre – but the cap had been so near the surface I didn't think it necessary to go further. Panting slightly, glowing with exertion, feeling very much better indeed, I surveyed the jagged rectangle in the turf. And then I began to put it all back.

I was in the bath when Mum went through to the kitchen to put the kettle on. Sam was still on the phone to Lisa, but they had finished talking seriously and were sharing a crossword.

Mum called, 'What's that you're singing, Matt?'

I hadn't realized I was singing. I listened to myself, then said unwillingly, 'It's the "Runaway Train".'

Mum laughed. 'Sounded like the wailing of a ghost,' she said through the bathroom door. Then added lovingly, 'But a very happy ghost.'

I wondered if there were such things as happy ghosts. But nothing could spoil my mood just then. My flu had disappeared, there was no body buried on the sea wall, and when I told Lisa she said quietly, 'Thank you, Matt.'

Hilda said, 'You're doing OK, Savernack. You ran like a racehorse on Saturday.'

Remembering Lisa's scathing comments I said, 'But we lost, sir . . . Hilda.'

'Yes.' He looked over my head thoughtfully, 'That was a bit of a bummer.' He looked down at me and grinned. 'Trouble is, only one side can win. It just so happens that up till now that side has not been ours.'

'No.' It was a bit too deep for me but I grinned back.

'Tell you what.' He turned to leave. 'Let's set ourselves a goal. Before the end of the season, we'll be the winning side.' Then he added, 'Make sure that Lisa Jenkins turns up. Everyone plays better when she's around.'

I watched him cross to the Sixth-Form block. I thought Lisa stood quite a good chance of becoming Prime Minister. But my money was on Hilda.

I said, 'Look, Dad. It's not that I don't want you to visit him. It's just that Lisa has set up a kind of interview and he might not co-operate if you're there too.'

'Interview?' Dad opened his eyes. 'The old chap is in no state to give interviews, Matt! If it's something to do with a school topic – Kingscote's history – you can go to the library.'

'It won't be there. This is something personal to him.' I sighed. 'I don't think he'll tell me anything, but Lisa says he needs to get it off his chest and he'll talk to me.'

'Why?'

'Don't know. 'Cos Sam and me are train buffs? Because of our grandfather? I just don't know.'

'Well, make it snappy. I'll go and get some shopping in, but then I want to get home.'

'Yeah. OK. Well . . . come on in when you're ready. He won't say anything.'

I trailed into the men's ward, caught Sister's eye and flattened myself against the wall.

'Good afternoon, young man.' She actually smiled at me. 'No more grievous bodily harm, I hope?'

'Sorry, Sister,' I mumbled.

'I got over it quickly. And I don't think I've seen Mr Jenkins laugh before.'

'Well . . . good,' I said, and waited for her to pass me before I moved down the ward. And then I paused. Because the curtains were around Mr Jenkins's bed.

One of the old chaps in dressing-gowns saw my hesitation – they didn't miss a trick – and called, 'It's all right, my boy! His granddaughter's with him!'

That still did not explain the curtains, but it enabled me to twitch them and say, 'Can I come in?'

Lisa pushed them back with her false hand. No glove or long sleeve today. She looked as raw and scoured as the Somerset Levels after a storm. And she had been crying.

I glanced from her to the bed. The old man looked fine. He was sitting up in bed, one veined hand resting on a tin box, the other on Lisa's skirt where her knee would have been if she'd had one.

'Wossup?' I asked, ready to back out immediately. 'Shall I go?'

'No. Don't do that, boy.' The old man's voice

was stronger too. He looked as good as – better than – before the stroke. Get yourself a chair. We've been waiting for you.'

Lisa glanced at me. She looked totally miserable. It was a new expression to me and I was pretty horrified.

'There's no room for another chair. And Gramps needs the curtains around. I'll move up and you sit on the bed.'

We fidgeted about, arranging ourselves. The curtains wound themselves around my legs and Lisa pulled the material out impatiently.

'Why bother?' I asked, trying to hide my legs under the bed.

'Gramps doesn't want the other men hearing anything.'

Normally she would have spoken sarcastically, because although the curtains shielded us from view, they did nothing for muffling sound. But she spoke drearily. As if she didn't care.

Gramps said briskly, 'Are we settled? Wonders will never cease.' He leaned back on his pillows and looked at me from beneath beetling brows.

'She wanted me to talk to you, lad. Thought it would be easier for me – man to man, stranger to stranger. But she's the one who has to know.' He frowned suddenly. 'You're here as a witness. D'you know what that means?'

'Yes. I can verify that you have said what . . . whatever you say.'

'That's about it. Isn't it, Lisa?'

'Yes,' she said dully. 'But . . . it doesn't matter any more, Gramps.'

'It matters. It matters to me and it will matter to you. So pay attention, girl!'

She looked up fleetingly and half smiled, 'Yes, Gramps.'

'Good lass.' He put his free hand to her face and cupped her cheek and she turned her head and kissed the palm. I swallowed fiercely. I thought of Lisa, so disabled, being left. Of Gramps taking her on. Of the amazing relationship they must have built over those years.

He said quietly, 'I'm so proud of you, I could bust sometimes. D'you know that, girl?'

She nodded dumbly.

He had his hand on her shoulder now; I could see he was holding her hard.

'I want you to be proud of me in the same way.'

'I am, Gramps!' It was a cry of protest.

He shook his head. 'You love me. You wouldn't care if I *was* a murderer—'

'But that's good! That's how love should be!'

''Course it should. But you don't have to love me like that, Lisa. Because I'm not a murderer.'

'Gramps – I know that! It's you – you've always taken the blame in your heart – you know you have—'

'Yes. For a time. For the rest of the war I did.

But then . . .' He turned his smile on me. 'I asked your dad to fetch me that proof I told you about, boy.' He patted the tin box. 'It's here.' He looked at the box. 'I wasn't going to tell anyone about this ever. Lisa could have found out when I was gone. But then I thought . . . why not share it with her while I can? Why not share it with the two of you? Let you get used to the idea – chat it over. Yesterday's news.' He sat forward slightly. 'Nostalgia don't they call it? All the rage, I understand.'

'Gramps—' Lisa was suddenly anxious. 'You mustn't overdo—'

'All right.' He subsided against the pillows. 'I'll get on with it while I've got the strength.' He closed his eyes, but he still looked OK.

'That night. The night of the disaster. I was twenty. I'd been reserved – that means I didn't have to go into the army – but all that changed when the proper war started.' He opened his eyes and smiled at us. 'It was called a phoney war at first, you know. Nothing happened. Our drivers and firemen volunteered, but I'd just got my job and the cottage that went with it. So I stayed put. But I got my call-up papers that day. The day of the storm. I had to report to Corsham four days after Christmas.' He closed his eyes again. 'At any rate, they drafted a train crew from the Great Western to run the coal. Bert Hadley. Frank Mayhew. Stanley Jeavons.' He nodded slowly. 'Good enough chaps, I suppose. When you got to know them. But not like the old crew. They weren't local.'

He hoisted himself up in bed slightly.

'It was Bert. He was the one. After all the girls. And he was married with two kids. Showed us snapshots, he did. Lovely kids. He was the one what started it.'

There was a long pause. Lisa said, 'Started what, Gramps?'

'The plan, Lisa. The plan.' He sighed. 'I should'a stood against it, 'course. I see that now. But then . . . they were older than me. And from the town. I thought perhaps everyone went on like that.'

'Go on, Gramps,' Lisa encouraged gently.

'Yes. Well. He reckoned she were nagging him to death. Making his life a mis'ry. He had to get away from her. And there was this girl down Yeovil way, reckoned she was expecting a baby by him . . . Oh, you young people don't know what that was like. Shame. She could have been tarred and feathered even. They're a funny lot over the Mendips. Any rate, he reckoned he thought a lot of her. So he worked out this plan.' Another sigh. 'On the last trip – around midnight it were timetabled – he would leave the train straight after it crossed the Cote Stream. I would be waiting for him with a bicycle. He would skedaddle towards Yeovil. The other engineman would report he had fallen into the river. I would find his cap as evidence the next day. He would be presumed dead and his wife would get his pension.'

'The – the dirty old man,' Lisa breathed.

'Aye. It meant I had to report my bicycle stolen . . . all sorts. I was brought up Baptist. I didn't like it.'

'No.' Lisa nodded. 'No, you wouldn't.' She glanced at me. 'He's so honest. I told you, didn't I?'

I nodded too. But there was a long way to go.

'Well, I was out and about most of that day. Getting my bike along to the bridge. I already had one of his caps and I stuck it in the bank where the tide would give it a good washing and I could pick it up. That's how come I missed old Gaffer. But 'course, one of my jobs was to make daily examinations of the bridge and when I did it late that afternoon, it was plain to see it weren't going to hold up against the storm.' He shook his head slowly. 'That were the worst storm I've ever seen. The flakes of snow were like pebbles. They bruised your face . . .'

Lisa said, 'Could you telephone or something? Let them know the bridge was unsafe?'

'I had a morse tapper in the cottage. I sent message after message. No way of knowing whether they got through. I don't think they did. Probably everyone had gone home in that weather – it was crazy to send the train off for the sake of a single trip.'

'So you were fairly certain there would be no train that night?'

'Ninety-nine per cent certain. But just in case, I turned out at eleven o'clock, crossed the bridge, walked half a mile down the track and put my hand lamp on to Danger.'

'The wrong side of the bridge . . .' I couldn't resist murmuring.

He opened his eyes. 'The right side, boy. I was trying to stop the train going on to the bridge.'

I said, 'Yes, but . . . Gaffer Baker saw you on this side. With your bike.'

'Yes, boy. With my bike,' he said emphatically. 'Just like he said.' He held my stare and I looked away. When I looked back his eyes were closed.

He said, 'I couldn't believe it when I saw the train approaching. And going at least thirty-five too. She never did more than twenty-five, even in good weather. I stood there, waving my blasted lamp like a maniac. Only just got off the line in time. I had to jump for it in the end. Went crashing down almost under the driving wheels. An' of course, when I got myself up, picked up the lamp, the train was on the bridge.' He took a deep breath. 'I prayed it would hold. After all, it had been rickety for years. And Jerries had been bombing the area for ages by then. If it had been going to collapse, wouldn't it have done it before then?' He moved his head slightly and answered his own question. 'She were going too fast. The blizzard and the strain . . . the bridge went. Right in the middle. The train seemed to buckle in at the third coal wagon. Made a V-shape as she went down. She hissed and spat – could see it from where I was. Then nothing.'

His hand on the tin box was white.

He said, 'I went mad then. Really mad. I ran back and jumped off the bank into the water, still holding me lamp—' He smiled ruefully. 'P'raps if I'd left it where it fell they might 'a b'lieved me at the inquiry. But the current was strong. It was swept out of my hand. Never saw it again. And I never found any of them. Bert. Stan. Frank. All gone.' He opened his eyes. 'It were a nightmare that were. I never thought I'd get out of the water myself. One thing saved me. I'd marked a place on the bank. Where I'd hidden the cap. Marked it with a piece of old rope tied into a tree root. And that rope was floating on the water. And I found it.' He opened his eyes and looked at Lisa. 'And the cap.' He grinned. 'I felt . . . I felt that cap had saved my life. That's why I gave it a ceremonial burial. 'Sides, it were all that were left of my mates.' His mouth tightened suddenly. 'Or so I thought.'

He began to fiddle with the clasp of his box.

'You know all the rest. The inquiry. What happened. An' 'course, I couldn't tell 'em about the plan. Else Bert's wife might 'a lost out on her pension. So I just kept quiet and let them think what they wanted to think. And they wanted to think the worst.'

The clasp opened and he lifted the lid of the box. It was full of papers.

'That's my Last Will and Testament,' he said, leafing through. 'Them's the deeds of the house. That's your father's birth certificate and wedding certificate. And this . . .' he brought out a letter. 'This is my proof.'

He tossed a plain buff envelope across the bed in my general direction. I picked it up and held it sort of helplessly in mid-air. I could see it was addressed to Mr H. Jenkins, Little Kingscote Halt, Somerset. Our address. It didn't make sense.

Lisa said, 'Open it, Matt. Read it to us. That's what you want, Gramps, isn't it? For Matt to read it to us.'

'Ah.' He spoke with some satisfaction. 'That's what I want.'

I eased the paper out of the envelope gingerly. Things fall to pieces in my hands and I knew this was a very important document. Not that it looked important. The paper was ripped off a notepad raggedly, and it was like the recycled kind we get now with all bits in it.

I flattened it on my knee. There was a date at the top. 15 February 1941. No address. I began to read.

'Dear Harry,
    Sorry not to see you before we left. Hope you managed to pull it off for us. Tried to

reach you on the tapper, but no reply. Thing was, we all had our call-up papers that day. So much for being in a reserved occupation! No way was Frank and me going to go in no army. And Bert had other plans, as you well know! So we decided we'd go together. We stoked up the firebox so she'd run just over the bridge and tied down the dead-man's handle. You must have guessed what had happened when you saw that. And we made it look as if there'd been a fight – I tore my uniform and hung it over one side. It was a devil opening her up. Bert had to jump clear before she reached maximum speed. Bet she rattled over that bridge, didn't she? I don't know how they explained away me being on the footplate with Bert and Frank, but they wouldn't have been that interested. All you see in the papers is war, war, war.

Anyway, the best of luck to you, Harry. Perhaps we'll meet up one day, but I hope not! Don't split on us, will you? I had to let you know in case you thought we'd really copped it!

Regards, Stan.'

There was a long silence.
Then Lisa whispered, 'Oh, Gramps.'
I said desperately, 'Surely after the war you could have told the authorities?'

Mr Jenkins shook his head. 'They went after deserters for years, my boy. And anyway, I didn't get that letter until three years after the war had finished. They demolished my little cottage at the Halt and chucked all my stuff into cartons. When I was demobbed I was still . . . sore. I bought the house down on the beach and went to work in the bakery – I'd been a cook in the army, see. It wasn't till I'd met my wife and got married that we started going through all that rubbish. And I found Stan's letter.'

'But then – why not then, Gramps?'

'It were such a relief to me, Lisa, I didn't worry about anyone else. And not many people remembered the old Mushroom Line. And certainly they didn't remember the Board of Trade inquiry. But then the bungalow was built. Just on the self-same spot as my cottage. And your brother came to live in it.'

I met his eyes. He was smiling. He didn't often smile.

He went on, 'When Lisa told me about the train noises, I knew your Sam would have to find out all about it. I didn't want that. I tried to clamp down on the whole thing. Wouldn't talk to Lisa at all about it.'

She nodded.

'But then . . . when Lisa dug up that old stuff in the newspaper office, I got a bit worried. I put the letter in here with my will and things. So she'd

123

find it one day. But then . . . I wanted Sam to know. And that meant she had to know. And you too . . . as a witness. Will you tell him?'

I nodded too. I suddenly knew that neither Lisa nor I could speak. In case we cried. Why on earth we should feel like crying didn't make sense. But it was a fact.

We all sat there for a bit. The old man closed his eyes and kept smiling. I held the letter, staring down at that strange, grey, war-time paper with its faded brown ink. Three deserters. All that time ago. Landing a twenty-year-old lad right in it up to his neck.

Sister's voice sounded down the ward, talking to someone . . . Dad. Then she said loudly, 'And what do you think you lot are doing all round Mr Jenkins's bed like that?'

I turned and pulled back the curtains with a jerk. Four elderly men in brown dressing gowns were standing right next to us.

Mr Jenkins opened his eyes and started to laugh.

'Now you all know!' he crowed. 'You all know what happened!'

Sister started shooing them away, but he was still laughing when she returned.

'My goodness, that's the second time you've had Mr Jenkins in stitches,' she said to me in a congratulatory voice.

Dad stood there, smiling at the three of us. I wanted to fling myself at him as if I were six years old again. Cling to him desperately so that no-one – nothing – could split us up.

He said, 'Ready then? I'm taking Lisa up to Automobiles to pick up her lift.'

I cleared my throat. 'Ready, Dad.'

And Lisa looked up, very bright-eyed.

'Ready, Mr Savernack,' she said.

After all, this was 1993. Fifty-three years is a long time.

Fourteen

Sam was not as excited as I'd thought he would be.

'Isn't it funny,' he said, smiling, slapping his dead legs gently as if he expected to wake them up. 'It all seemed so complicated. And awful. And when you find the answers to things, it's so clear and straightforward. And simple.'

'It doesn't sound very simple to me,' I protested. 'Poor old Jenkins trying to flag down that train – watching it go over—'

'But then when he got the letter—'

'Eight years later.'

'Yes. Those must have been horrible years for him. But then . . . it was all right. And almost funny. So – so simple.'

'But he couldn't tell anyone. That's what makes it awful. He had to keep that secret until now.'

'He need not have done. He could have left it – say – ten years—' Sam grinned. 'He wanted to have a secret. Like us.'

I grinned back unwillingly. We still hadn't told Mum and Dad. It would mean having to tell them that Grandad's trainset had worked all by itself without electricity. They wouldn't be able to swallow that. Perhaps when they were as old as Lisa's gramps . . . perhaps you had to be young or old to believe things like that.

Sam's grin widened. 'It's going to be great to get a full night's sleep again,' he said.

The funny thing was, the other train – the one we could hear but couldn't see – went through as usual at midnight. Mind you, we were so used to it, we barely registered it. And after all, it took no time at all.

It was definitely the best Christmas we'd ever had. Mum asked Lisa if she would like to join us, but they were having a big party at Thornbury and her gramps was being taken there in a hospital car, so she opted to stay put. She asked to speak to me.

'Hi, Lisa.'

I was in the best possible of moods. The last day of term we'd had a game against the Firsts. They were all twice our size and Hilda was a giant. But we didn't do too badly. I'd scored a touchdown. They'd carried most of us back into the dressing-room on their shoulders. It had been like a riot except all the teachers grinned and cheered us instead of handing out detentions. I knew that I liked Kingscote Comp. I liked living just outside at Little Kingscote. I liked living on an old railway halt. I liked . . . just about everything.

Lisa said, 'You sound cocky.'

'So do you.'

'I always do. You don't.'

'Come off it. I've had a lot on my mind.'

'Well, now you needn't worry about my family any more.'

I paused. She might sound cocky, but I suddenly sensed she wasn't feeling cocky at all.

I said cautiously, 'Your gramps OK?'

'He's in hospital after a stroke. Won't come out again. Yeah. Fine.'

'Lisa. Sorry. You know what I mean.'

I heard her sigh with exasperation. 'You put your foot in it quite often, don't you, Savernack? What between knocking out hospital Sisters—'

'Lisa—' I pleaded.

She said – amazingly, 'Sorry.'

I didn't know how to cope with Lisa Jenkins when she was being nice. I remember holding the receiver away, staring at it with sheer disbelief. She had never apologized to me before and I was willing to bet she'd never apologized to anyone in the whole of her life before.

She snapped suddenly, 'Close your mouth, Matt. You look like a guppy.'

How had she known my mouth was open? I closed it and mumbled, 'Sorry,' too.

She said, 'I asked to speak to you so that I could wish you a merry Christmas.'

I suddenly saw the light. She'd wanted to accept Mum's invitation, but it would have been barging in.

I said quickly, 'Lisa. Please come here. Your gramps can come as well—'

She interrupted me with a laugh.

'Stop trying to ruin my life, Savernack!'

My jaw dropped again. 'What are you talking about?'

'You know very well I'm trying to educate myself for my destiny in life!'

And she put down the receiver.

I held on to it my end, wondering just how tough Lisa Jenkins really was. I'd probably never know for certain.

But I did know that Sam liked her. And she had been a good friend to me. Sometimes.

Mum said, 'You look like a cat who's got at the cream!'

I nodded. 'I think I am,' I said.

All the usual things happened. Cards and hiding presents from each other and going with Sam to Automobiles to see a special pantomime and spending a morning with the Prices, making up a stocking for Mum and Dad. When Sam had learned about Father Christmas two years before, he had been completely undismayed.

'If it's something they do for us, then we'd better do it for them too,' he'd said to me. 'That'll give them a surprise, won't it?'

And it had been a complete surprise that first time. Without Grandad's help, they'd known we were hiding things. But this year, doing it at the Prices, they wouldn't know a thing. We put in some hard-boiled goose eggs which Sam painted, and chocolate cigars for Dad and bubble bath for Mum, and our 'big' presents. A pullover for Dad chosen by Mum, and a jumper for Mum chosen by Dad.

When the train went through at midnight on Christmas Eve and we were in that no-man's-land of no-time, we took Mum's and Dad's stockings into their room. Sam sat in his chair, holding the door back so that I could make a quick exit, but in fact we could have shouted the place down; we knew only too well that those two or three minutes were frozen as long as we could hear that train. It had its uses. We got back into our bunks just as the sound rumbled around the sea wall into silence. We were both giggling. Dad's voice came sternly from the other room, 'Go to sleep this minute, you two! It's only midnight!' We stifled our laughter somehow. At the bottom of the bunks our lumpy stockings lay ready. We just hoped Dad wouldn't spot his and Mum's. But there was silence after.

On Christmas morning, we woke up at six o'clock and opened our presents and then took them into the conservatory to try out on the track. Yes, they were model trains. Sam had one of the new hi-tech tamping machines. I had a Pullman coach.

We knew when Mum and Dad woke up because Mum sort of screamed with delight and then her voice came down the hallway, 'When did you two do all this? Dad – look – a goose's egg— Can you believe it!'

Dad said, 'Egg-and-cress sandwiches for tea!'

Mum said, 'Turkey sandwiches today!'

Dad said contentedly, 'Tomorrow then. They'll keep. Look at the size of them! I haven't had an egg like this since I was Sam's age.'

They were more thrilled with the goose eggs than with their jumpers. Sam grinned at me and I grinned back.

After breakfast we went down to the farm. The Price family had homed in from all corners of the country. Jessie and her husband Ron with their twin daughters who did everything together, especially crying; Maureen and Janette who were backing singers to a group we'd never heard of; and Derek who was an independent financial adviser and had to get back to London that night for a big party his wife was organizing.

It was like being in the middle of the geese when they started honking at each other. Everyone wanted to talk to Sam and stroke his hair and say wasn't he sweet. Sam caught my eye now and then and sent me terrible messages, but mostly he took it pretty well. And it was only for an hour while Mum and Dad downed sherry and we had ginger wine and mincepies.

The we were out in the lane again with the big grey winter sky like a tent over us and the sea nudging gently at the wall the Italian prisoners of war had built, and the prints of the Mushroom Line where no real tragedy had ever really taken place. A happy railway line. I remember thinking that. A happy railway line.

Dinner was great. Mum wore a new apron which said, 'Handle with Care', so Dad kissed her under a sprig of mistletoe, then we settled down for the Queen's speech while Sam had his sleep.

And then we went for a walk. I think that was the best part of all. Dad and I trundled the chair up to the top of the wall and we could look across to the Holme islands and just see the dark hump of Wales. We walked right down to the Cote Stream and stood there, gazing into its muddy chasm.

Mum said, 'Look at this square of fresh earth. Somebody must have done this quite recently. I wonder what it's all about?'

And, quite suddenly, Sam and I had had enough of secrets and we started to tell Mum and Dad about old Jenkins and how he had buried the cap there that terrible night in December 1940.

Dad said wonderingly, 'That's what he was on about at the hospital, was it, Matt?'

I nodded. 'Lisa was so worried about him. She thought that *he* thought he was a murderer!'

'Yes. I can understand that. I remember that day he came to see us. He just stared out of the conservatory window as if the place was haunted.'

Sam and I were suddenly silent and Mum said

sharply, 'Why did he want you to know? I don't understand that part of it. How did you get involved in the first place?'

Sam looked up at me. We weren't certain about this part. About whether Mum and Dad could take it.

I said cautiously, 'We . . . sort of . . . heard things. And it was like a game. A detective game. We had to try to find . . . and Lisa joined in . . . and it seemed to involve her gramps . . .'

Dad said, 'When we started digging the garden. We were turning up old fishplates—'

'But the cap.' Mum's voice was still sharp with anxiety. 'You must have known where to look for the cap. I remember when you came home that day – filthy—'

Sam said truthfully, 'That was an accident, Mum. We had a bit of an argument and Matt kicked at this molehill – ant hill – and we found bits of cloth and then the brim and the badge.'

'And then you were so ill,' Mum concluded.

Sam said matter of factly, 'And then I got better. Because I wanted to find out what had happened—'

'But now you've found out!' Mum crouched suddenly by his chair and stared right into his face. 'You've found out, Sam. And that's an end to it.'

It was strange; she sounded stern like she always did when she was telling us what to do, but there was also a sort of pleading note in her voice.

Sam's gaze flicked up and met mine. We accepted

our midnight train now as a matter of course. But we knew Mum would not.

Sam nodded. 'And it was a good ending,' he said. 'Because it made Lisa's gramps happy. Matt said he laughs quite a lot now, and he never did before.'

Dad said, 'That's true, love.'

Mum smiled suddenly and stood up. 'Well . . . that's something, I suppose.'

We started back and Dad pushed the chair like a dodgem car in between all the sea-wrack and Sam made engine noises and Mum and I followed behind.

Mum said, 'Imagine Lisa's gramps actually seeing the train go into the river and thinking that three men were going to their deaths.'

'Yeah,' I said.

'It must be such a relief to him that Lisa knows the truth. Like laying down a heavy load. After all these years.'

'Yeah,' I said.

'And it was good that you and Sam could help him to put down that load. Grandad would be pleased about that. It's almost as if Grandad and Sam between them . . .'

'Yeah,' I said.

She was silent and I thought perhaps the subject had been dropped. I should have known better.

Mum took my arm suddenly in a grip that hurt.

'No more detective work, Matt. D'you understand me?'

'Of course. Anyway, there's nothing else to find out.' I crossed the fingers of my free hand. The train was still running invisibly along the old Mushroom Line.

She said, 'I mean it, Matt. Sam's not up to it. You know that as well as I do.'

I said no more. I knew it. We all knew it. But we never spoke of it.

Fifteen

We played three matches in January and Lisa did not turn up to one of them. I knew she was winding me up by her silence. I went to see her gramps twice but both times he was asleep and Sister told me I'd 'just missed that wonderful little granddaughter of his'. Lisa would have spat at that.

Then, at the end of January, it began to rain again. For two days it did not let up and parts of the water meadows behind the sea wall flooded to a depth of fifteen centimetres. Mum was worried it might affect us. Dad went to see old Mr Jenkins and had better luck than me.

'He says his little cottage at the Halt never once flooded,' Dad reported.

Mum was only partially comforted.

'Maybe they never had rain like this.'

'How was he?' I asked. 'He's been asleep when I've gone in.'

'He's very weak.' Dad looked grave. 'Lisa is going in practically every day.'

That accounted for her not coming to my rugby

matches. But surely she could have dropped by to see Sam?

'She did turn up at Automobiles one afternoon,' Dad said, anticipating my question. 'But it was the day Sam was having his check-up and neither of us were there.'

That night the rain became visible through the darkness and we realized suddenly it had turned to snow. I felt about five years old.

'We can get out the toboggan!' I yelped, tearing mindlessly around the conservatory. 'We can go down the sea wall! We can make a snowman! We can have a snowball fight—'

'Sam can't go out in it,' Mum said in the kind of voice that brooked no argument.

Sam said, 'Mum—'

'And that is most definitely that!' Mum added for good measure.

'I was only going to say, I can watch Matt from in here.'

Dad and I stared at Sam as if he'd grown horns. We'd expected him to wheedle Mum around the way he always does. Unless this was his latest ploy. Agree with her and it would worry her so much she'd practically throw him out.

But if so, it didn't work.

'Good lad,' she said and switched off the train so that she could go into the kitchen. As she passed his chair she put out a hand to touch his shoulder. Sam was not demonstrative and that was all he would allow. But this time he reached up and touched her fingers fleetingly.

The snow was so deep there was no school. And it kept coming down, too. Dad and I went out to shovel a path through to the lane. We met Mr Price coming towards us on the tractor. He'd got a couple of plough shares fixed on the front to scoop the snow into the ditches.

'What about the ducks?' I shouted above the roar of the engine.

Mr Price yelled that they'd opted for their nests under the willow tree.

'Heard about old man Jenkins?' he bawled as we turned to go back to the bungalow. 'Died. Early hours.'

I stared at Dad and we both broke into a run. But we were too late. Mum was in the bathroom, taps turned on; Sam had answered the phone. He was still holding the receiver and there was a tear quivering slightly on the end of his nose. He looked up and saw that we knew.

'They're here now. Will you talk to Matt?'

I held out my hand but he shook his head and then replaced the phone carefully.

'She doesn't want you to hear her crying,' he said.

I could believe that.

'Is she all right? Was she there? Where is she now?'

'Yes. She was there. She's back at Thornbury now.' He looked at Dad. 'She doesn't want us to go to see her.'

'We'll go anyway,' I said, looking at Dad. 'She can't be there on her own all day.'

Dad said, 'She's not on her own, Matt.' He put a hand on Sam's shoulder and the other on mine. 'That's why she went to Thornbury. So that she'd have plenty of people.' He frowned. 'Also, her father tries to keep in touch. Perhaps now . . .'

I was amazed. 'I thought she was an orphan.'

'No. She blamed her father for her mother's death. But he'd left them ages before that.'

Somehow that shut me up. Lisa was a constant surprise. That's how she liked it; that's how she made her restricted life exciting. But this was one of her secrets that also made her seem so . . . beleaguered. Lisa alone, battling through life like Boadicea with no arms, was a splendid figure. Lisa running from a no-good father was something else.

We did our best with the snow, for Sam's sake. By teatime there was a gigantic snowman on the patio outside the conservatory and Dad had made Mum's clothes line into a tall semaphore signal and stuck up a sign that said 'Little Kingscote Halt.'

'He's waiting for the midnight train!' Sam crowed through the glass.

'What did he say?' Dad asked me.

'Nothing. Something about the snowman waiting for a train.'

'That kid! He's train mad!' Dad laughed comfortably and switched on the outside light so that we'd be able to see our small snow set-piece while we had tea.

And Lisa did not phone again.

'Was she crying a lot?' I asked Sam almost nervously when we went to bed.

'No. She just kept saying, "Where will he go now?" – things like that.'

'What did you say?'

'I said perhaps our grandfathers will be together.'

'And what did she say?'

'She said she just wished she could know he was happy. That's all.'

'Yeah.'

Wasn't that what we'd all like to know?

I woke before the rumble of the train had started. Sam was manoeuvring himself out of his bunk and into his chair.

'Lavatory?' I whispered, hanging over the edge.

'No. Go to sleep.'

'What?' I was, of course, wide awake at that.

'I want to see something.'

'What?' I repeated irritably.

'The train. I want to be in the conservatory when it goes through.'

'For heaven's sake! Get back into bed . . .' I was already tumbling out myself.

From the other bedroom Mum's voice called anxiously, 'Are you all right, boys?' And before I could answer, the rumble started and time stood still. Mum's voice was cut off. Everything held its breath.

I snapped, 'It's snowing and cold. You're just asking to get another attack of bronchitis!'

'Don't be daft. You know this is a special time. You can't get bronchitis at midnight at Little Kingscote Halt!' He was bowling through the door as he spoke. I grabbed my slippers and a blanket and dashed after him as the train started to come down the track from the Prices' farm.

Dad had left the outside light on and the scene outside was somehow reassuring and eerie at the same time. It looked just as it had looked at teatime when we had sat at the table munching toast and making up a silly monologue for the snowman to say. Yet, it was no longer teatime. In fact, it was no-time. And the train was coming closer.

'Sam—' I tried one more protest, though I knew it was hopeless. Sam had something in mind and when that happened he was like a bulldog with a mouthful of postman.

The rumble was under our feet; I felt it as never before. My body hummed with the power of it. It was like standing too close to the edge of a platform when a high-speed train went hurtling through a station. I was going deaf . . . my head was coming off . . .

I glanced at Sam, expecting him to be cringing with hands over ears. But he wasn't. His face was rapt. He was gazing out at our snow scene as if it had suddenly become animated.

I looked up and saw why. A train was clanking down our garden.

I know I could be locked away for saying that. But there it was. Sam had seen it before me. It must have burst out of the ground just beyond the patio.

It was a goods train; a steam-hauled goods train. The fire-box door was pulled open and the sound of shovel on coal was quite clear even through the double glazing and the other train noises. In the sudden leap of flames, the driver was silhouetted. He was leaning out of the side of the footplate. He was waving. He was joined by his fireman. He waved too.

And then the train trundled around the bend in the sea wall and was gone.

In the silence that followed, Mum's voice was raised again and the next minute she appeared in the conservatory doorway.

'What on earth d'you think you're playing at?'

Her anger was directed at me and I was completely without words.

But Sam wasn't. He was as cheerful as a robin.

'I wanted to say good night to the snowman, Mum,' he explained. 'Sorry.' He grinned. 'Matt's been nagging me, and now you . . .'

Mum frowned and stood aside as he bowled past her.

''Night, Mum,' he called.

She looked at me.

'What's going on?' she asked.

I sighed, 'I wish I knew.'

She hustle-bustled us both into bed and made a thing about tucking us in.

'For goodness sake, use what small amounts of common sense you have!' she said to us both before going back to Dad.

Sam hissed through the darkness, 'You'll be able to tell Lisa, won't you?'

'What?'

'That her gramps is OK! That he's with our grandad! That we saw them both driving the Mushroom train!'

'You're mad,' I said flatly.

Lisa would either laugh me out of her life or be deeply angry.

But Sam was right. It had been Grandad. He'd been driving the train. And Lisa's gramps had been firing for him.

Sixteen

Of course, Sam knew Mum wouldn't let him attend old Mr Jenkins's funeral. That was why he'd given me the job of telling Lisa what we had seen that night. The snag was, she would have listened to him: never to me.

The snow had almost gone the following Friday and the cemetery which overlooked the sea at Kingscote was patchy like a Dalmatian dog. The wheels of Lisa's chair kept slipping in the slush, but she wouldn't let anyone help her. She was wearing her cloak with the hood well up. Her face looked very small.

I tried not to listen to the words; I remembered them from Grandad's funeral and I hadn't liked them. But I couldn't shut them all out. '. . . cut down like a flower . . . as it were a shadow . . . in the midst of life we are in death . . .' They suddenly had some meaning. I thought of the flowers growing all around the Mushroom Line; I thought of the shadows we saw and heard in our up-to-date, functional bungalow; I thought that last night, in the middle of our lives, we had found ourselves also in the middle of death.

I lowered my head and pushed my hands down into my duffle pockets. What did it all mean?

Jack Martin's mum had opened up the little house by the pier, cut sandwiches and made tea. There were a lot of people crammed into the living-room, which was a relief – there was just no chance of talking to Lisa privately. But I was hearing things she wouldn't want me to know: the details of her day-to-day living – Mrs Martin getting her into bed, the district nurse swinging her into the bath. I felt as if I were eavesdropping.

So I went through the kitchen and down the long, narrow garden. There were ramps everywhere; Gramps had made the garden accessible to Lisa at every point. I wondered what they had talked about, how they had managed together. Sam had three of us; Lisa had had one old man. But they had made a good pair.

Her voice behind me made me jump.

'You know this is my house now, do you?'

It was an aggressive question, but, unexpectedly, the voice was gentle.

I turned and looked into her pinched face.

'Gramps left everything to me. Enough money – just – to supplement grants and things so I can go to university. And this house.'

I said lamely, 'Will you be able to keep it?'

'Of course!' She looked fierce again, thank

goodness. 'This is my castle! I could hole up here for months!'

'Then . . . that's good.'

'Yeah. Yeah. It is, isn't it?'

She looked so forlorn I knew I had to tell her.

'Lisa—' I began desperately. 'Sam wants me to tell you something.'

'I'm not in the mood for romance . . .' She tried to sound like her old self and failed. 'What? What's that oddball thinking up now?'

If anyone else on earth had called my brother an oddball . . .

I said, 'Last Sunday night . . . just before the train went through—'

'It's still going through?'

'Yes. Every night. Same time.'

She said, 'No wonder you can't win a football match!'

I didn't smile.

'It was the day we heard about your gramps. Just before midnight Sam got up and went into the conservatory.'

'Why didn't you stop him? He could have caught his death of cold—'

'I couldn't. He was . . . in another world.'

I had her complete attention. Her eyes dilated.

'Go on.'

'We saw the train. We actually saw it. The small banker – the coal wagons – it seemed to slow right down at the Halt – where the Halt used to be – and then the fireman stoked the furnace and – and – we saw—'

There was a pause.

She said, 'What did you see? Quick, Matt! Someone will come out!'

'We saw . . . oh God!' It felt as though the wind had frozen my lips together. I had to force them apart. 'The driver was our grandad. And the fireman was . . .'

Someone came out and called to us about the cold and needing soup and sandwiches.

Lisa's eyes were shining now.

She whispered, 'The fireman was my gramps. That's what you saw. Didn't you?'

'Yes. I didn't want to tell you – upset you – but Sam said you had to know—'

'You idiot! As if that could upset me!'

Mrs Martin was coming down the path, looking cross.

Lisa said swiftly, 'Say thanks to Sam. I'll ring—'

And we were flapped back into the house like the Prices' ducks.

She rang and talked to Sam for ages. When he handed the phone to me, he was smiling.

'She wants a word.'

She sounded tired.

'I've talked for too long, Matt. I wanted Sam to know how happy I was. About the train.'

'I don't get it,' I said flatly. 'We saw something . . . peculiar. And that has made you happy.'

'I needed to know – positively – that he was happy. Gramps. And of course he is. There's no other way he could have told me. It's so simple, isn't it?'

'I don't think it's simple, Lisa. Why is it happening to us?'

'It's happening to Sam. Not you. You're just there.'

'I still don't get it.'

She sighed deeply and I waited for the sarcasm. It did not come.

She said slowly, 'It's an honour, Matt. Believe that. Because you're so close to him. And you always will be. Believe that too.'

She put the phone down gently; it hardly clicked against my ear. I turned and saw that Sam was watching me.

He said, 'Did she explain?'

I was suddenly so angry I was shaking.

'No, she didn't. I don't know what's going on!'

He looked mildly surprised. 'Nothing is going on, Matt. Did you think there was another secret?'

'Another secret?' I sounded as thick as I felt.

'Like the buried cap and the bridge collapsing?'

I suppose that is what I had thought. A mystery. To be solved.

I clenched my hands to stop the shaking.

'She said it was an honour.'

'Well then . . .'

I wanted to shout at him and then run into the kitchen and fling myself on Mum and cry and cry.

I said, 'I'm going to bed. Don't wake me when the train goes through. I've had enough honour to last me a lifetime.'

But I was awake at midnight as usual. Neither Sam nor I spoke a word. But we were both awake.

The following week, Sam's chest started up again. He moved in with Mum and Dad came in with me. The doctor mentioned hospital again.

Mum said, 'What's the point?'

The doc said, 'I'm thinking of you and your husband. And Matt.'

'We need to be together,' Mum said briefly.

'So be it,' said the doc.

I'd never heard anyone use that phrase before. It's often in books, but people don't go around intoning, 'So be it.'

I went in to see if Sam needed anything before I left for school.

He did not sit up.

'No thanks.' His breathing was horribly loud. 'Did you hear the train last night?'

'No.'

'Nor me.'

'I didn't hear it when Dad was in your bed before,' I said consolingly.

'No. Perhaps it only happens when we're together.'

It was as if a load had lifted from my shoulders. I hadn't thought of that before. All we had to do was to sleep apart. When Sam was better I would sleep on the couch in the living-room. And that would be that.

He said forlornly, 'I miss it.'

And I said . . . why on earth did I say it . . .? 'Just because you can't hear it, doesn't mean it's not there.'

He smiled, happy again. 'Thanks, Matt.'

I went to school. Everyone acted as if I were an invalid. I suppose Jack Martin told them about Mr Jenkins's funeral.

That was a terrible time. The place full of nurses, Mum looking awful, Dad trying to act as if nothing was wrong, Sam in a kind of coma.

'Keep talking to him,' they said. So when I got in from school I would do just that. And he would smile as if he heard me and move his small hand on the sheet in a kind of mini-salute.

I wanted so much for him to be well again that I took up praying. I always feel an idiot when I pray out loud. But I had to try everything.

There were gales at the beginning of February and one dark grey, furious morning we could see the spray leaping above the sea wall. Mum nearly let Sam go into hospital that day because she was afraid the bungalow might flood. But when she mentioned it to the doctor, Sam suddenly opened his eyes and said, 'No!' very clearly. And sure enough, as the tide went out, so did the storm. By dusk it was very still, very peaceful. The sky crouched over us, exhausted; the trees leaned away from the sea. I climbed the sea wall and looked at the grey humps of the Holmes. They lay doggo, keeping their heads well down.

I felt a surge of peace. As if everything was going to be all right.

I went back into the house and made toast for tea. Dad came in and said Mum was sleeping. Sam was, too. They looked as if they had been washed by this sudden peace.

Dad and I ate our tea standing up by the sink.

We were all so tired.

Seventeen

I have to write this bit very quickly. Just write it.
Don't think about it. Get it down as it happened.

So, OK. This is how it happened.

Dad came to bed about eleven and I whispered,
'Are they all right?' And he whispered back, 'Still
sleeping. Like babies.' And I smiled into the darkness because there would be no train to disturb any
of us and we could sleep as long as we liked. It was
Saturday the next day. No rugby. Just Saturday.

I woke to hear Sam's chair barging down the
hall.

At first, I thought I was dreaming. Then, when
it went into the conservatory, I sat up, alarmed,
wondering why Mum wasn't calling. I fumbled for
the light and looked at my watch. It was twelve.
No train sounds. Nothing. But it was twelve.

Dad didn't budge, light or no light. I slid to
the floor and chased out into the hall. It was as
black as a hat. I stubbed my toe on something and
kept going, a hand on either wall. The living-room
door was open. I skirted the sofa, knocked my other
toe, felt for the telly and put my hand out for the
conservatory door. It was open.

'Sam?'

And then it happened.

The patio was suddenly illumined by a white-blue light. Moonlight, I thought at first. But it was coming from the ground.

In the light I could see Sam, leaning forward in his chair, opening the outside door.

'Sam – don't – too cold—'

He didn't hear, which wasn't surprising because my voice was soundless. I started forward, but my bashed toes seemed not to move on the carpet. I was only halfway across the conservatory when Sam got the outer door open. At the same time, right at his feet, there was an enormous gout of steam, pale silver, ethereal, and the train emerged. First the sturdy bank engine, pulling slowly up what was evidently a terrific bank beneath the house; then the old wooden coal wagons, jerking and following the engine in a series of buffer-jarring leaps.

The train pulled to the bottom of the garden. And then it stopped. As if a signal were against it. The amazing thing was, all this happened completely silently. My ears tingled, waiting for the burst of jarring, hissing sound. None came.

In the strange light, Sam was now silhouetted. I saw him absolutely clearly. It was no shadowy, flickering hallucination. The train was silent, but it was there. Sam was silent too, but he was there.

He was leaning right forward, his hands braced either side of the outer door. As if . . . as if he was about to pull himself upright and stand free of his chair.

And that is exactly what he did.

He did it so easily, without any apparent effort. And then he just stood there for probably half a minute, looking down the garden at the train which was waiting for him.

I managed at last to break that silence.

'Sam!'

It was only a croak but he heard it and turned. His face was one big grin. Huge. It went from ear to ear. He looked so excited. And he was tall. I don't know why he was so tall. His legs still dangled uselessly. But he was tall. And then he laughed.

I croaked some more.

'Sam! Don't go!'

He said, 'Don't be daft, Matt. It's not for long. In fact – it's no time at all!'

And then he turned. How could I stop him? How could I do anything but be glad that he was free, moving without using his legs, flipping around Mum's whirly clothes line, reaching up into the engine.

Grandad leaned out and pulled him up. They both waved. And then they were gone.

When I woke up, Dad told me that Sam had died in the night.

I had slept through it all. The doctor arriving and Mum and Dad sitting with him.

Dad said, 'Don't be hurt, Matt. He went in his sleep. If he'd been awake we would have fetched you.'

'It's OK.' I hung my legs over the edge of the bunk. My toes were purple. 'It's OK, I said goodbye to him.'

Dad said, 'Well done, old lad. Well done.'

They thought I was being brave. And when I tried to tell them about the train and not needing legs, they thought I was going mad.

And maybe I was.

It was the last game of the season. Lisa was there. So was Hilda. We were playing the Avonmouth Giants. It was only the third game since Sam had caught the train and I knew we were going to win.

So did Hilda.

'You left it a bit late,' he said as we roared off the field. 'But let's look on it as a start for next year.'

'OK.'

I grinned up at him. I could have told him about Sam and the train and he would have listened and not called me a liar or a loony. But after all, it had been an honour, and it wasn't really on to go around boasting about it.

I didn't need to tell Lisa.

She said, 'Write it down. Write it all down from the time you first heard the train. Everything. So that when we're quite old and forgetful we can read it and find the important thing.'

I said, 'I know that already.'

She looked at me with a new respect.

'What?'

'It's about time. That it's non-existent. That there's no time at all.'

She said slowly, 'I hope you're not really going crazy, Matt.'

'Why?'

She said very seriously, 'I won't be able to give you a job in the Cabinet. When I take office.'

I started to laugh. Whatever happened now, it was going to be great. I really must try to convince Mum and Dad of that.

I let them read this.

I think they're convinced.

THE END

ABOUT THE AUTHOR

Susan Sallis is the bestselling author of a number of previous titles both for adults and for young readers. Her best-known novel for young readers is *Sweet Frannie*, which won the American Library Award and was a runner-up in the Young Observer competition in 1982. Her adult novels include the popular quartet about the Rising family – *A Scattering of Daisies*, *The Daffodils of Newent*, *Bluebell Windows* and *Rosemary for Remembrance*, all of which are published by Transworld.

Part of the inspiration for *No Time at All* is drawn from Susan Sallis's lifelong interest in railways, her grandfather, father and husband all having worked as railwaymen.

She has three children and two grand-daughters and lives in Avon.

JOE AND THE GLADIATOR
Catherine Cookson

What with trouble at home between his parents, and trouble with a bully at the shipyard where he works, life is pretty bleak for fifteen-year-old Joe Darling. Then an unlikely friendship with an old rag-and-bone man, Mr Prodhurst, leads him into the greatest challenge of his life. For Mr Prodhurst bequeaths Joe his peculiar-looking horse, The Gladiator – with only enough money for a couple of weeks feed! How can Joe possibly look after the horse properly? He is determined to try. Otherwise, The Gladiator will have to be put down . . .

A tense and absorbing tale of one boy's courage and determination to succeed against all the odds.

0 552 52617 7

A SELECTED LIST OF TITLES
AVAILABLE FROM CORGI BOOKS

THE PRICES SHOWN BELOW WERE CORRECT AT THE TIME
OF GOING TO PRESS. HOWEVER TRANSWORLD PUBLISHERS
RESERVE THE RIGHT TO SHOW NEW RETAIL PRICES ON
COVERS WHICH MAY DIFFER FROM THOSE PREVIOUSLY
ADVERTISED IN THE TEXT OR ELSEWHERE.

☐ 52751 3	**HACKER**	*Malorie Blackman*	£2.99
☐ 52527 8	**GO TELL IT TO MRS GOLIGHTLY**	*Catherine Cookson*	£2.99
☐ 52617 7	**JOE AND THE GLADIATOR**	*Catherine Cookson*	£2.99
☐ 52141 8	**LANKY JONES**	*Catherine Cookson*	£2.99
☐ 52526 X	**MATTY DOOLIN**	*Catherine Cookson*	£2.99
☐ 52528 6	**MRS FLANNAGAN'S TRUMPET**	*Catherine Cookson*	£2.99
☐ 52525 1	**OUR JOHN WILLIE**	*Catherine Cookson*	£2.99
☐ 52725 4	**BILL AND THE MARY ANN SHAUGHNESSY**	*Catherine Cookson*	£2.99
☐ 52717 3	**THE BOY WHO WASN'T THERE**	*K.M. Peyton*	£2.99
☐ 52707 6	**COOL SIMON**	*Jean Ure*	£2.99

AVAILABLE FROM ALL GOOD BOOKSHOPS